THE SHOOT-OUT

"You can back out of this any time you want, kid."

"It was you who started it. You back out." Waldo's voice was easy, and there was a cool confidence that makes a man's blood run cold.

"Why don't both you boys break it up?" a voice from the crowd rang out.

But neither Waldo or the other fellow paid any heed to that.

"I'm giving you one last chance to back down with only an apology, kid."

Waldo swept back the tails of his frock coat, unruffled, and casually extracted a cigar from an inside pocket. He wetted it between his lips, then grinned around the cigar and reached inside another pocket for a match.

"Well?" the fellow demanded. "What will it be?"

"Take your best shot, peckerwood."

"You sonuvabitch." The man's hand inched for the gun, but since Waldo was in the middle of lighting up a smoke, the fellow took a more deliberate approach and rested his hand upon the grip of the Colt, waiting.

Other *Leisure* books by Douglas Hirt:
BRANDISH
McKENDREE

A GOOD TOWN

DOUGLAS HIRT

LEISURE BOOKS   NEW YORK CITY

With much appreciation to
Kristen Heitzmann and Mary Davis
Wonderful writers . . . great friends . . .
and darn good copy
editors!

A LEISURE BOOK®

August 2001

Published by

Dorchester Publishing Co., Inc.
276 Fifth Avenue
New York, NY 10001

ISBN 0-8439-4861-2

Visit us on the web at www.dorchesterpub.com.

A GOOD TOWN

Chapter One

"Tink!"

Catching my breath, I leaped off the board-walk and raced up the street, slumping to my knees at his side. I blinked back sudden moisture and hardly noticed the desert wind, or the dust that stung my eyes.

"Tink!" I put an arm under him and pulled his head up onto my legs. My hand was suddenly warm, and when I looked, blood dripped through my fingers. Out the corner of my eye I saw Alice running up the boardwalk. She stopped abruptly and clutched at the porch upright as if her knees had gone weak. The hot wind had pulled her hair loose and whipped it across her wide, staring eyes. There was horror in her face, and she must have seen the same in

7

mine as I looked back at the man in my arms.

"Tink," I tried again. There was no response at first, then his eyes fluttered and came open. They seemed not to see me.

"Tink, I'm here."

"I . . . I know," he managed. "Did . . . did I get him?"

My glance went down the street. Waldo Fritz hadn't moved. Tall and still slender after all these years, Waldo's gaunt face grinned at me as he slowly slipped his revolver back into its holster. He took a cigar from an inside pocket of his frock coat and turned it between his lips. He seemed to be waiting.

I looked back at my friend and shook my head.

Tink coughed, and his eyes rolled up some. "Not surprised . . . Waldo always faster than me . . . than you . . ."

"Why did you do it?"

He half grinned. "You know why, Howie. It's . . . it's always been my job, watching after you," he wheezed.

"Don't talk." I glared into the crowd beginning to gather around. "Someone get a doctor!"

Tink clutched my arm with a sudden urgency. "Too late for that." His eyes shifted toward Alice. "She's a good woman, Howie. Don't . . . don't let Waldo ruin her with his . . ." A ragged cough carried off the rest of what he wanted to say. When it passed, a smile moved across Tink's blanched lips. "I'm gonna be all right— soon. You . . . you take care, old friend . . . lousy birthday present . . . sorry. This definitely is not a good town," he rasped as his eyes closed.

I cradled Tink's head, and in those few moments my thoughts went back more than a dozen years—back to Bisbee, when Tink and I were but fresh-faced kids—back to that day we first laid eyes on Waldo Fritz. . . .

"Hey, Howie, where are you going?"

I stopped on the boardwalk in front of Kasper's Hardware Store, surprised to see that Dobie Tinkerman had just stepped out of Bench's Saloon across the street. He waved an arm at me and skipped across the dusty street, avoiding the road apples with a practiced step. With a spring to his feet, he easily leaped the eighteen inches to the boardwalk.

"Hi, Tink," I said with a grin and nodded at the saloon. "What were you doing in *there?*"

At that moment a man stepped out of Bench's. He was tall, with a cut-granite face beneath his wide gray hat. He wore a long, black frock coat that seemed too large for his beanpole frame, and when he reached inside it for a cigar, the butt of a Colt's revolver peeked out. I couldn't help but stare. He was a gunman, I could tell that much. We never saw many of his kind come through Bisbee. But what struck me most was his youth—no older than Tink or myself. He stepped off the boardwalk and, to my surprise, started across the street toward us.

"Who is that?"

Tink glanced over. "Oh, him? His name is Waldo Fritz. We just met over Bench's new billiard table."

Waldo Fritz stepped up beside us, whipped off his hat, and patted his sweating forehead with the sleeve of his jacket. "Blasted hot day," he said, levering the hat back into place over matted black hair. He grinned at me. "The name's Waldo," and he stuck a hand out. I took it. It was bony, like the rest of him, but I sensed a certain strength in it—the kind a man develops from doing the same job over and over again.

"This is Howie Blake. The fellow I was telling you about."

Now, that made me wonder.

"Where are you heading, Howie?" Tink went on.

"Up to Deavers, to help Ma carry the laundry home."

"I'll walk with you." Tink used his hat to beat

the dust from his trousers and shirt before setting it back on his head. He gave Waldo a nod, and the two of them fell into step with me.

"How come you aren't at work?"

Tink made a face. "I sneaked out of the skip shack before the second shift went down. I hate that blasted hole. Feels like I'm dropping down into Lucifer's lair ever' time I step into the skip. Actually, Waldo and me was just talking about it."

I glanced at the tall stranger in time to see a thin smile slide like hot butter across his face, then he looked away from me. Waldo's face was like mine in only one point: Both of us had but fine peach fuzz to cover our chins. It was embarrassing at times. I figured him for about my own age, or a year older. Eighteen tops.

"What will Carlyle do if he finds you skipped out again?"

"Probably fire me," Tink said with a brashness I had not heard before, and again I found myself looking at Waldo. The gunman was staring off across the street at Margot's Palace. I was stunned at his open curiosity. Ma always made me turn my head aside when we passed that place.

"Fire you?" I stopped and studied Tink. "What has got into you, Tink? Those prospects don't seem to trouble you much."

He laughed. "We've been through this before, Howie. You just wait until it's your turn. You've been lucky so far, what with your folks making you stay home to watch the girls and all. I started at the mines when I was fourteen. But your turn is coming—in fact, considering what day today is, it won't be long before your ma packs a lunch bucket for you like she does your pa. Then you'll learn real quick what mining life is all about."

I shuddered a little at the thought of that, careful not to let the older boys see my fear. That was a day I lived in dread of. I'd watched my father grow old and crippled-up before his time because of the mines, with nothing to show for his work but a rented company house, an empty bank account, and a wife who worked twelve hours a day so that the family could make ends meet. No, I had no desire to follow in his footsteps.

"Anyway," Tink said, "if I do get fired, it will only give me an excuse to part company with this dusty town. There has got to be something better out there somewhere—something more than digging a hole and getting yourself blown up or crushed to death in the process. There has got to be a good town somewhere out there for me . . . and you too, Howie, if you're smart. Who knows, maybe I'd go to San Francisco, or maybe Chicago. Waldo here has been to Chicago, ain't that right?"

Waldo pulled his eyes from Margot's Palace and allowed that it was true.

"Really?" I tried not to sound impressed. "What was it like?"

Waldo shrugged his narrow shoulders as if it was a small thing. "It was all right, I reckon. Lots of people around, and a real big lake."

"Did you see the El?" I asked, recalling a picture in a magazine I'd once seen of the new electrified elevated railway.

"The what—? Oh, yeah, I seen it," he said quickly. "It weren't much to look at, though."

For a moment my head swam with the notion of going off to Chicago, and seeing the sights and all. Then reality hit me and I was frowning again. "I don't know, Tink. Ma still needs my help with Anne and Beth."

"That ain't gonna last much longer," he said.

We walked on. I knew he was right, and today of all days, the truth of it rang home loud and clear, like the steeple bell atop the First Presbyterian Church.

"And by the way," Tink went on as if he had read my thoughts, "happy birthday."

"Thanks." I grinned a little. I was seventeen today, more than a man in most circles. The grin faded. It wasn't going to be long before the

girls were old enough to take care of themselves, and then just as surely as night comes to
day, it would be my turn in the mines.

Then I noticed something and stopped again,
staring at Tink.

"What's the matter?" he asked.

"What is that you have got growing there?"

"Where?"

"There, on your chin, and above your lip."

Tink frowned. "Ain't you never seen a beard
before?"

"Not on *your* face, I haven't."

Waldo bent over for a look and grunted his
approval.

I said, "When did you start growing it?"

Suddenly Tink was embarrassed. "Over two
weeks ago," he mumbled.

"How long?"

"Two weeks," he barked, daring me to make
a comment.

And I almost did, but I caught myself. After
all, who was I to judge? I couldn't grow even a
little beard if I wanted to. Not in two weeks—
not in two dozen. "It's coming along nicely," I
allowed.

"It is not either. You're just saying that. You
hardly noticed it at all."

"I reckon I hadn't 'cause it is so light
colored—like your hair."

"Maybe if I rub some boot black into it, folks will—"

"Think you've got a dirty chin," I finished for him.

Tink frowned. "I reckon you're right." Then he was grinning again. "It'll get darker with age," he said confidently, "they always do." Dobie Tinkerman was a fount of optimism, and it was impossible not to catch some of it at times.

We turned into Deavers' Laundry and old man Deavers glanced up from his paperwork at the jingle of the bell. Kent Deavers was about as tall as me, but he had a thirty-pound advantage if he had an ounce. He'd long ago lost his hair, and his face seemed to hold a perpetual crimson glow about it, as if he'd been boiled like a lobster. He'd always been partial to me, and Ma said he was a fair man to work for.

"Well, if it isn't Mr. Blake and Mr. Tinkerman," Deavers said, tucking his chin to peer over the top of his spectacles at us. "And who is this young fellow?"

"Waldo Fritz," Tink said. "He just got into town."

Deavers looked Waldo up and down, saw the six-shooter, and didn't offer his hand.

"I've come to help Ma," I said.

Deavers hooked a thumb at the doorway in

15

back. "She should be about done back there. Go on through."

The room was steamed up like an Indian sweat lodge, and smelled of soapy water, dirty laundry, and bleach. Ma was bent over a black cauldron, swirling the gray water with a flat paddle.

"You're early, Howard," she said.

"It's nearly four o'clock."

Ma straightened up with some difficulty and looked surprised. "Not already?" She glanced around the cluttered room at the piles of waiting laundry, a look of despair coming to her tired face. "Will I never see an end to all of this? I should really stay another hour—but not today." A strand of limp hair had fallen over her left eye, and she brushed it aside. "I've got your birthday dinner to prepare, Howard." Her spirits seemed to lift some, and she smiled at Tink. "You are coming to dinner tonight, Tink?"

"Well, I don't know . . ."

"Do come, Tink," Ma insisted.

"Well, all right, then."

Ma noticed Waldo. "Who is this?"

"Waldo Fritz, ma'am," Waldo volunteered, suddenly remembering his hat and grabbing it off his head.

"Tink met him over at—er, in town today. He

16

is just in from . . ." I looked at Waldo. "Where is it you are from?"

"Douglas, ma'am," he said as if my Ma had asked the question. "I'm on my way to Tucson."

"You're alone?"

"Yes, ma'am."

"Well, then, you come to dinner too. We have plenty."

"Why, that is kind of you, ma'am. I would be pleased."

Before I had time to say yea or nay, it had all been arranged. We helped Ma empty the big cauldron and hang clothes on the line in the fenced yard out behind the laundry. When we had finished, Ma took her cane from the back of a nearby chair and, leaning her weight on it, went out into the main room. I grabbed up the basket with our personal laundry and followed her.

Deavers was still squinting at the ledger books.

"I'll be leaving now, Mr. Deavers," Ma said.

"And you got you a couple fine fellers there to help you on your way, I see."

"There are still piles of dirty clothes back there. I will be in early tomorrow."

"It ain't going nowhere, Mrs. Blake." Deavers took a green, paisley money purse from his desk drawer and removed four coins. "Here you go. Two dollars."

"Thank you." As Ma put her pay into her purse and returned it to her bag I couldn't help but notice her red and chapped hands. It was the soda crystals in the wash water that dried them out so badly. She rubbed Vaseline into them every night, but she could not afford to stay away from her work long enough for them to heal properly. And all for two dollars a day. I thought of my father's rough hands, and the two fingers missing from an ore car accident nine years ago—more than half a lifetime ago. All for three dollars a day. There had to be a better way to make a living.

Waldo seemed to be studying something on Deaver's desk. I didn't think anything of it at the time. We all went outside. Tink and Waldo angled off across the street, promising to be at the house by around seven. I knew that Tink was vaguely uneasy around my family, but he was friend enough to come anyway, and that was important. I wasn't sure how Waldo would take to them.

I hefted the basket to my shoulder and Ma and I went home to our clapboard house at the edge of town.

Chapter Two

The three of us were sitting on my front porch, watching below as the evening shadows lengthened out across all of Bisbee—a collection of crooked shacks staggering down a hillside to crowd around the main street that ran past a row of more permanent structures. I was staring off at all the tin roofs, not really seeing them, listening to Tink and hardly believing what I was hearing.

"I tell you, Howie, I am giving it some careful thought. You know like I do that there ain't no future for us here. Look at me. I started working at the mines when I was fourteen, and now I'm eighteen and my back hurts most all the time and my knees ache, 'specially when the weather takes a turn. If I stick around too long, the mines will cripple me up like they've done to half the men in town."

I glanced at him, but my eyes really went past Tink to Waldo Fritz, who was twirling his six-shooter and grinning. "Maybe so, but are you going to up and leave your friends and family because some stranger you just met over at Bench's tells you the grass is greener over Tucson way?"

Waldo's grin lengthened.

In his defense, Tink said, "Waldo didn't say it was any greener, only that it was a place to have a good time, and maybe make some money. Ain't that right, Waldo?"

"That's what I said. I'm not twisting no arms, Howie. You and Tink can come along or not as you please."

I gave Tink a skeptical look. "It don't sound right to me," I said, but inwardly the prospects were exciting. It was true, Bisbee was a dead-end town right from the get-go.

"Well, it sounds all right to me. I figure if I throw in with Waldo, the money will come along sooner or later. And if it don't, well, at least I'll be away from here, and out from under the thumbs of shift bosses like Carlyle."

I moved my feet on the rough boards of the porch, feeling restless, and stared past the tips of my dusty shoes on the second step down. It was not so long ago that my feet only reached the first step.

The dirt path beyond the steps led to the road, nearly lost in the growing night. Down the hill, the lights of Bisbee were beginning to brighten the grimy windows of a hundred little shacks exactly like the one we lived in. If the townspeople knew of such a thing as paint, like my pa with liquor, they certainly did not indulge in it. Bisbee was altogether as drab and dry as the southern Arizona real estate it occupied. And only now, with night coming on, was there any relief from the awful heat.

"You'll be back, Tink," I said finally.

He only laughed. "Nothing but a pine box will get me back here."

"What about your ma and pa?"

The blaze dimmed a bit in Tink's eyes, his grin faltering. "Well, maybe I might come back for a visit, but that's all. I'm gonna find me someplace exciting to live, Howie."

"Chicago?"

Tink shrugged. "Can't say where I'll end up. I'm not ruling out anyplace until I see it."

"I'll miss you." At that moment I wanted with all my being to join Tink in his adventure, but that was impossible.

"You can come along, Howie . . . if I really do decide to go."

21

Douglas Hirt

"Yeah, Howie," Waldo put in, "we can have us a grand old time, you, me, and Tink. Shoot, I'm just traveling by myself. Besides, three of us can do a whole lot more than just one."

I wondered what he meant by that, and I considered the offer for an instant, then the dark cloud of reality drifted over and cast its shadow on the plan. "No, not so long as Ma needs me to look after the girls while she's away to work."

"How much longer is that gonna be?" Tink said. "Anne is almost eleven, and Beth is already fourteen. Shoot, they're old enough to look after themselves now."

"I was on my own when I was thirteen," Waldo said, spinning the cylinder of his revolver near his ear just to hear it click.

I grimaced. It was true. The girls were almost old enough to fend for themselves, and once they were, I'd not be needed to help watch over them. That should have made me happy. It didn't. This birthday I was seventeen, a man, and expected to carry my own weight. That meant only one thing in Bisbee. The mines.

"Howard! Tink! Waldo! Dinner is ready," Ma called from inside the house. It was a welcome interruption in a conversation that was feeling more and more like an overstarched shirt. We got up, and Tink grabbed a brown paper sack at his side. Waldo unbuckled his gunbelt and hung it over the saddle horn of his horse, which was tied to the porch railing. As we went inside, I wondered why I so bitterly rejected the work that Pa seemed to enjoy. But the prospects of spending my life scraping hard rock into a bucket to make another man rich just held no appeal to me.

Our house was dirt plain, and I figured Waldo had seen lots better in his travels. It wasn't but a square box, twenty feet to a side with one main room for cooking, eating, and receiving guests. There were two doors set into the back wall. The girls slept in the room behind the door to the right, while Ma and Pa used the other. I just stretched out in this room, on a sagging sofa covered with a quilt to hide the threadbare upholstery where cotton stuffing spilled out like dirty snow.

Ma was at the stove and the girls were already sitting around the sturdy oak table. The house had not given off the day's heat, even with the windows all open. The odor of roasted venison, sage, and boiled potatoes lifted my spirits some. There were, after all, some benefits to having a birthday. Ma didn't usually buy venison steaks, and there was even a frosted cake sitting on the sideboard. Iced cakes were a treat reserved for special occasions.

"John," Ma called, and after a moment Pa

emerged from the back room, folding an arm through a suspender strap. He had put on clean, neatly patched trousers, and a white shirt with pale blue pin-lines. It was well worn, but clean and freshly pressed. I hardly even noticed the new patch Ma had sewn onto the right elbow. Pa was wearing a new paper collar tonight, and as he came into the room, I thought I smelled spiced toilet water. Pa never used toilet water except on Sunday mornings when it was his turn to stand in the doorway of church and shake the hands of the folks as they came in. It occurred to me just then that I never remembered Pa taking such pains to look so dapper at any birthday celebration—not even for the girls.

"John, please carry the venison to the table," Ma said, and turned an eye to my sisters. "Beth, come carry the potatoes."

"Yes, Mama." Beth was the oldest, and already she cooked for the rest of us when Ma was at work. She also cleaned the place as best she could, but there was just so much that could be done with unpainted boards and exposed timbers. The rough floor ate up straw brooms at a furious rate.

"I want Tink to sit by me," Anne said happily, patting the chair at her side. Anne was always laughing, showing those nearly perfect teeth, and playing with her braids of fiery red hair that traced back to Pa's great-aunt Sadie.

Tink grinned. "Well, that would be a real honor, Miss Blake," he said, drawing back a chair. Then, giving me a wink, he said, "It has been such an awful long time since I've pulled a pretty gal's pigtails that—"

"You better not, Tink," Anne said, dragging the two long braids over her right shoulder and out of his reach.

Beth said, "Aw, he's only funnin' with you, Anne."

"Sit down, don't be shy, now," Ma said to Waldo.

"Thank you, ma'am," he said, taking the chair next to me. Somehow, I didn't picture Waldo Fritz as the shy type, and I wondered if he wasn't only pretending to be.

The meal was set out, the family gathered around, and when Ma hooked her cane over the back of her chair and sat down, a sudden hush settled about the table. I stifled a small cringe and knew what was coming next and why Tink had hesitated over coming to dinner. In a moment Pa would say grace and give a litany of all of our blessings. What blessings? A house where the wind blew a mountain of dust through the walls? A larder that was nearly always empty? Never enough money to properly clothe my sisters? A job that put a man's life in peril every day he went to work? As far as I was concerned, there wasn't a whole lot to be thankful for.

"John, will you please bless the meal?"

"Yes, dear. Let's all join hands."

Why did we have to hold hands when company came to dinner? I thought. Wouldn't a simple bowing of our heads do well enough?

Pa's sandpaper hands folded about mine. They were hands that had suffered mightily in the copper pits. On my other side, Waldo Fritz's hand was soft and undamaged by hard labor. I stole a glance across to Tink. His head had tilted forward and he was accepting our family ritual without a fuss. That, at least, was some comfort.

Pa blessed the food and affirmed all that he was thankful for, and when it was over the hardest part of the evening was past. Bowls and platters started around the table.

Pa said, "Today is an important milestone in your life, Howard."

I concentrated on the thick brown gravy I was pouring into the crater in the center of my potatoes and didn't respond to that.

Across the table, Tink stabbed a slab of venison steak, transferred it to his plate, and held the platter for Anne as she took some. "I keep telling Howie it's time he gets himself a real job."

I wished Tink hadn't said that.

Pa grinned at Ma, and the two of them exchanged something in that look—something I didn't quite catch, but it made me suddenly uncomfortable sitting there beneath their knowing gazes.

Ma passed the potatoes to Beth. "I can't tell you what a big help Howard has been to me these seven years."

Seven years! Had Ma worked for Deavers that long? I counted it up in my head and realized it was true.

"He has grown into a good man," Pa went on, scraping peas onto his fork with a knife.

Their conversation made me feel as if I had suddenly become invisible, or had died and was overhearing the artificially kind words people were supposed to say at a funeral. I tried to steer the conversation to a different track. "Tink is thinking of heading up to Tucson."

"Is that right?" Pa set his fork down and looked interested. "What is over Tucson way?"

Tink shrugged. "Oh, I don't know, Mr. Blake. Waldo and I were talking it over some."

Both Ma and Pa's eyes shifted toward Waldo Fritz, who was busy cutting his meat, pretending he hadn't heard.

"Hmm," Pa said finally, and there was a note of disapproval there. "What about your job here, at the mine?"

"There are lots of jobs around," Tink said, stabbing a carrot with his fork.

"Maybe, but you got a good one now."

Tink gave a short laugh. "Reckon I could do better if I work at it."

Pa considered the food on his plate a moment. "Is that why you skipped work today?"

Tink nearly choked on the carrot. He swallowed it down hard. "How did you know about that?"

"Oh, I heard Carlyle say something about one of his drill men not showing up for his shift. I thought I heard him mention your name."

"I, ah . . . I was seeing to other business."

"Important business? Important enough to risk your job?" Pa glanced at Waldo, who looked up just then and gave a pleasant smile, as if he'd just been handed a compliment on how neat he looked.

Tension settled heavily over the table, and Anne squirmed in her chair at Tink's side, seeming to sense it too.

Ma cleared her throat. "Oh, they wouldn't fire Tink for skipping out once in a while. It's not the first time someone has played hooky from the mines." She glanced at Pa and raised her eyebrows. "And I'm sure it won't be the last." Ma made it into a joke and laughed. The mood lightened, and Waldo and Tink laughed too. Pa only smiled, and he knew Ma had just warned him to drop it. And he did.

We ate our way through dinner and into dessert, and afterward Ma and the girls cleared the dishes and poured coffee. Tink reached under his chair for the paper sack he'd brought with him and said, "Happy birthday, Howie."

In the bag was a new, black leather belt, with a Mexican silver buckle like one I'd admired down in Nogales last spring when we'd crossed the border to see the sights.

"Thanks, Tink. This is great!" I shed my old, battered belt and donned the new one.

"Happy birthday," Waldo said, and I thanked him.

Ma had a bundle hidden behind her back, and she handed it to me. "Happy birthday, Howard." She and Pa watched me unwrap it. I was careful not to rip the printed paper, which I knew had been an extravagance for them. It was a new shirt, with a paper collar like the one Pa was wearing.

"Gee, thanks."

Ma said, "We thought you might need a new shirt—now."

"Now?"

She looked to Pa, who was struggling with a grin. "I talked with Mr. Patch last week, Howard."

I had a sudden sinking feeling. Cornelius Patch was one of the bosses for the Phelps Dodge company.

"He wants to hire you on at the Copper Queen, Howard. You'll start as a mucker at two dollars and fifty cents a day. I've arranged for you two to meet next Monday."

"But . . . but . . ." My brain was whirling faster than I could keep up. That sinking feeling had become a dizzying plunge. "But what about the girls?" I stabbed frantically. Tink's prediction was coming true, and I was desperate to clutch at any straw to divert this gloomy prospect. Life at the mines, as far as I was concerned, was about as deplorable as life in jail. Maybe worse!

"With you working now, Howard, I can quit my job at the laundry."

What could I say to that? Ma worked her fingers raw to help the family, and here was her chance to leave all that. I sat there, unable to speak. They both saw, and Ma's eyes turned worried, but Pa only grinned wider and said, "It's not the end of the world, Howard. You'll learn to like the work after a while."

"Yes, sir," I replied, and after that the rest of

the evening was a blur. It wasn't until a couple hours later, after the party was over and I was standing by the gate to our yard with Tink and Waldo, that the fog began to lift.

"Boy, Howie, to see the look on your face, I thought for sure you were planning to find the nearest tree and use that new belt to end it all." There was a laugh in Tink's voice, and I grinned for the first time since Pa had broke the news. Tink was the sort who could find humor in an old bedpost if he wanted to.

"I wasn't even thinking *that* clearly," I said.

"Tough break, Howie," Waldo sympathized. He was twirling his six-shooter around his finger and snapping it out every now and again as if pretending to shoot at a lamp or lighted window down in town.

"Five to one you get Carlyle for a shift boss," Tink wagered. I didn't much care for the crooked grin he gave me, or the way he said it. I frowned.

"I'm going into town," Waldo announced. "Want to walk along?"

We both nodded, and I shut the creaking iron gate. We took the alley down past the darkened windows of the Lucas Furniture building and out onto the main street.

"You ever see a steamboat?" Waldo asked, breaking the silence.

31

"No," I said.

Tink looked interested. "Have you?"

"Oh, sure. They are all up and down the river at Yuma. Must be thirty or forty of 'em there all the time. You can hear those steam whistles miles off. Sort of like a locomotive, but higher in pitch."

"Gee, you've been everywhere, haven't you, Waldo?" Tink said.

"Been a lot of places. Still a lot of places left to see." He looked at me as if weighing his next words. "You know, Howie, you'll never see anything but the bottom of a deep copper pit if you stay here."

That was just what I needed to hear. My spirits had been on a very gradual rise, but now they plummeted again.

"My pa never told me what I was going to do with my life," Waldo went on. "He knew better. If he had, I'd have left home years before I did."

"But Ma—"

He broke me off. "How old is your ma, Howie?"

I shrugged. "I don't know. Thirty-eight . . . forty, maybe."

"Shoot. She's practically an old lady. Her life is already half over. Yours is just beginning. Besides, look at it this way. With you gone, it will take a whole lot less money for them to live on.

Whether or not you realize it, they'd be better off with you gone and on your own."

That sent a shiver up me, but the more I thought it over, the truer Waldo's words rang. They *would* be better off with me gone.

I could tell Tink was warming to Waldo. "He's right. I'm going to leave my family in a lot better position by going to Tucson. You come with us. We'll have a bully time, the three of us."

My thinking wasn't too clear right then, and that's always a bad time to go making life-changing decisions. A part of me was still scrambling for a way out, a way to put things back the way they were before this day. "But how will we live? I haven't got no money, and you hardly have any either, Tink."

Waldo gave a laugh. "Money is no problem. You stick with me and there will be plenty of money. I've got plans. Between the three of us, we'll be rolling in cash."

I liked Waldo's confidence. I'd never heard anyone talk with a swagger like Waldo Fritz could. Not even the old miners who'd sometimes stop by the house to play chess with Pa. Almost before I realized it, we'd turned a corner and were heading into Zacatecas Canyon. I stopped.

Tink and Waldo went on a few steps, then looked back.

"What is it?" Tink asked.

"This is Brewery Gulch!"

"Is that what they call the place?" Waldo said.

"You're not going in there, are you, Tink?"

"It's all right. Waldo and me had us a beer here earlier today."

"You? Waldo?" I had never been in Brewery Gulch. Ma and Pa had warned me of the place. *A den of thieves and the haunt of sinners,* Pa had declared on more than one occasion. Everyone knew it was a rough place, and the farther up the gulch you went, the rougher it got.

"Think we oughta?"

"Come on, Howie, it's okay," Waldo said confidently. "I've got some money. I'll buy us a beer."

Chapter Three

My heart was thumping like a parade drum and the palms of my hands were suddenly moist. Tink and Waldo slapped me on the back and said we'd have us a grand old time, and somehow, my feet started to move. I was gawking at the lights and men roaming the street, hearing honky-tonk pianos blare from a dozen different saloons. The scratchy music of an Edison phonograph wafted down from an upstairs window somewhere. There were women about too, loud and painted, draping themselves shamelessly off the arms of miners, and even *I* knew what sort of characters they were.

We turned toward one of the saloons, and Waldo pushed open the batwings and stood there looking around the place. He'd moved his coat aside so that his revolver was in plain sight. But no one seemed to notice him, and I detected a flash of disappointment in Waldo's eyes as he started for the bar.

"Think we ought to be doing this?" I whispered.

"It's okay, Howie." Tink nudged me through the doors. I didn't know what to do, so I just stood there staring. It was a busy place, with racks of smoky chandeliers lending a bright, festive light. Lots of men jostled for position at the long, polished bar. There was a brazen painting on the wall behind the bar, and I shifted my eyes away from it.

Waldo wove his way through the crowd, carrying three mugs with foam piled up high on them and sliding down the sides. He nodded toward a vacant table, and we settled in. I was still skittish, but the initial shock was wearing off. I peered cautiously at the beer Waldo shoved in front of me. I'd never had a beer. It looked tasty and smelled tangy. I'd encountered that smell only a few times before, on the breaths of other men. Never on Pa's.

"To success!" Waldo declared, raising his mug in a toast.

"To success," Tink and I echoed. This was all new to Tink too, but he pretended he'd been drinking beer in a Brewery Gulch saloon all his life. I gave it a try and made a face.

Tink laughed.

Waldo assured me that the flavor grows on you. He watched me sample it again and grinned as I wiped the foamy mustache from beneath my nose.

"Grow it any way you can," Tink quipped. I had to laugh. Beer was rather flavorful in its own peculiar way, I decided after giving it another chance.

"So, what do you think, Howie? You going to throw in with Tink and Me?" Waldo was sitting back in his chair looking like a man very much in control of life. I liked that.

"I don't know yet."

"It's either us or the mines," Tink reminded me.

I frowned and tasted the beer again, liking it better this time. I suppose I've made dumber decisions on the spur of the moment, but I can't ever remember when.

I wasn't feeling real good when I got back home early in the morning. A light was still burning in the house, and then a shadow moved behind the drawn curtain and I knew I was in trouble.

In a darkened corner, Pa looked up from the big chair that he liked to sit in when he was reading or thinking. He was dressed in his nightshirt, and I could tell he'd been worrying.

"Sorry I'm late," I said, quietly closing the door behind me.

"Where have you been, Howard?" came his low voice from the shadows. I couldn't see his face.

"Me and Tink, we were just down in town, hanging out." My words sounded funny to my ear, and the harder I tried to change that, the worse they sounded.

"Celebrating your birthday?"

"I . . . I reckon so."

"It's after three."

"I didn't know." I struggled to speak without breathing out much. I'd drunk four or five beers—until Waldo had run out of cash—and I knew I must smell like a brewery.

Pa stood and peered at me, his face coming into the light of the single lamp burning on an end table in the corner. "Well, at least you're home now," he said finally. I had the feeling he wanted to say more but was restraining himself. "You all right?"

"I'm all right."

"You and Tink out by yourselves?"

"Waldo was with us."

Pa's face tightened. I could tell Pa didn't approve of Waldo, and I braced myself for the lecture I figured was coming. But it never did. Instead, Pa just looked me dead in the eyes. "Well, you're old enough now to make your own choices, pick your own friends."

I wondered why that made me feel suddenly uneasy. I'd have almost preferred the lecture right then.

Pa looked at me for a long moment. "Go to bed, Howard. You look all done in." The flicker of a grin touched his lips and he turned and started for the bedroom.

I wanted to tell him right then that I'd decided to go with Tink and Waldo to Tucson. But the words wouldn't come out. I started, stammered, then said, "Good night, Pa."

I lay wide awake until dawn began to brighten against the window curtains. About the time I finally fell asleep, I was awakened by a sudden banging at the stove. The strong scent of brewing coffee filled our house, but I still smelled beer on my breath. I rolled over, my mouth drier than an old leather work glove, and looked at Ma. Her back was to me and she was flinging pots and cracking eggs, making more noise than usual. She had opened all the windows.

"You smell like a saloon, Howard," she blurted all at once, her back still toward me, somehow knowing I had come awake.

"Waldo bought Tink and me a beer, for my birthday," I said lamely.

The skillet clanked hard upon the stove.

"I never thought a son of mine—" She let that declaration ring in the air unfinished.

I grimaced and stood. My head hurt and I desperately needed a drink of water, but I didn't move, sensing there was more to come.

"That boy, Waldo, he's a bad influence, Howard."

"Waldo's not such a bad sort," I responded in his defense.

She wheeled around and glared at me. "Look at you."

I glanced in the mirror that hung near the door. I didn't think I looked any different from any other morning.

She turned back and began flipping over the eggs in the sizzling skillet. "I don't want you hanging around with that boy anymore," she continued. "And I have half a mind to march right over to the Tinkermans' house and tell them the sort of character Dobie has been associating with."

Ma never called Tink Dobie unless she was really upset about something. The bedroom door opened and Pa came out dressed in his wool and canvas work clothes. He took in the situation in a glance and kept his expression flat

40

and his thoughts hidden as he sat down at the table.

Beth and Anne's door had inched opened a crack, but the girls did not come out. They understood that when Ma had her fury up, it was always safest to keep clear of the storm.

"I didn't do anything wrong."

"We were worried sick last night. Then you come in after three o'clock, smelling like you've crawled through every saloon in town. And you say you didn't do anything wrong?" She wheeled and stared hard at me. "Howard, answer me this. Were you drunk?"

"No," I said truthfully. I might have been a little light-headed, but I wasn't drunk . . . at least I didn't think I was. But then, how could I be sure? I had nothing to compare it to.

"That's something to be thankful for, I suppose!" Ma spun back around to the frying eggs. She took up her cane in one hand, lifted the skillet with a hot pad in the other, and carried it to the table, where she filled Pa's plate. "Well, I don't want you seeing that boy anymore, is that clear, Howard?"

"I'm going to Tucson with Waldo and Tink," I blurted out. The house went dead silent for a couple heartbeats while I endured the discomfort of both my parents staring at me. I don't know why I had said it so bluntly, except I knew it was better to get it out now than to break the news to them later.

"That's not a wise decision, Howard," Pa said slowly when the shock wore off. "What about your new job? What about your mother?"

"I don't want to take that job, Pa. I don't want to work the copper mines. I never have. And with me gone, it will take less money to keep the house and feed the family. Ma can still quit her job at the laundry. You will all be better off with me gone."

Ma's eyes began to fill, but Pa's face remained unmoved, his voice lowering some. "Who ever put that notion in your head?"

"No one," I lied.

The door to the girls' room opened wider and Anne's wide-eyed face appeared in the gap, but both Ma and Pa were facing me and didn't see it.

I was miserable for having said it, but I was angry, too. I knew it was time for me to leave—time to shake the dust of Bisbee off my shoes and light out for a different town. Tink was always talking about moving away and finding a good town somewhere, and right then I determined I would go with him. We'd both find a good town. Maybe it wouldn't be Tucson. But somewhere out there we would find it. Waldo Fritz's arrival was only the spark we both needed to do the things we had talked about for so many years.

"It's not true, Howard. We still need you here," Pa said.

That only made my decision more painful. "I've made up my mind. We already have plans to leave."

"We?" Ma managed, strengthening some. She was still holding the iron skillet, forgotten for the moment and now apparently weightless. "That boy, Waldo, he's influencing you."

"No, he's not." That was another lie, but one I sincerely wanted to believe.

She grimaced. "When?"

"Soon."

Tink came by the house later that day.

"What are you doing here? Skipping work again?" I asked when he appeared in the doorway.

"Nope. No more skipping for me." He grinned. "I quit."

"Quit? Are you telling me the straight of it?"

"I am. Finally did it. And you should have seen the surprise on Carlyle's face. I'll bet he never had a man up and quit on him before."

"Then we're really going." I'd almost convinced myself that it was all a dream and I'd come to my senses in the morning, doomed to a life in the mines.

"Course we are, Howie."

We went around to the shady side of the house and sat on the benches that Pa and I had built two summers before.

"Where is Waldo?"

"He's buying a couple horses. We're gonna need transportation."

"With what money? He was dead broke last night."

Tink shrugged and kicked a pebble at a rusted tin can over by the edge of our lot. "I don't know, but he has a knack for making money, and if we hang close to him, so will we."

It sounded too good to be true.

"Didya tell your folks?"

A sudden heaviness pressed down all around me. "I did. They didn't like it."

"Yeah, neither did mine. But they'll get used to the idea once we're gone, Howie. I figure I'll send them lots of letters."

"And picture postcards from all the faraway places we get to." For some reason, the notion of keeping in touch with letters and postcards made me feel better.

Tink grinned. "Maybe San Francisco."

"Or Chicago."

"Or even New York," he suggested.

"I'd like to see the Statue of Liberty."

"We will," Tink said confidently, and I could almost believe it was going to happen.

I was feeling better by the time Tink left. Ma came home from work a little while later, and she was quieter than usual. Beth and I had gotten dinner started, and she took over. I told her I could finish, but she wanted to do it.

Pa came in about an hour after her, bone-tired and covered in dust, his cheeks and arms smudged, his hands sore and cracked. He soaked them in warm water and rubbed salve into them. That was practically a nightly routine around our house. He didn't say much either. No one said anything about my leaving, but I was sure the girls had discussed the matter between themselves. And Ma and Pa would have words long into the night over it. I was feeling bad again about leaving, but I knew my time had come and I had to go.

"I don't want Howie to go away," Anne blurted during the meal. Beth nudged her under the table, and Pa said, "None of us wants him to go, Annie."

Ma moved food around her plate distractedly. "The laundry was broken into last light."

Pa shook his head. "Broken into? What did the thieves take?"

"They got away with about seventy dollars.

45

Luckily, Mr. Deavers doesn't keep too much cash on hand."

Seventy dollars sounded like a lot of cash to me.

After dinner I was out on the front step watching the town darkening below, and counting the lights that appeared one by one. It was a pleasant evening, with a freshening breeze from the west. Because of our elevation, Bisbee never got as hot as Tucson or some of the other nearby towns. I heard the door open and Pa's heavy footsteps on the narrow porch. He sat beside me, resting his arms upon his knees and letting his hands dangle out in front of him.

"Howard."

"Pa."

"You do any more thinking on leaving?"

I nodded. "I'm going with Tink. He came by today. He quit his job."

"I heard." There was no judgment in his voice. It was merely a statement. "When are the three of you going?"

"Tomorrow." It hurt to say the word.

Pa was silent for a long moment. "Well, when a man gets to be your age he's got to do what is right for him. We'll miss you. You've been a joy to have around, Howard, and you have been a big help to your mother and me. We've done our best to raise you right. I know you will make out. And if you decide you want to come back, our door is always open."

"I know," I said softly.

He reached into his pocket and pressed something into my hand. It was a five-dollar gold piece. "You might need it."

"But you can't afford—"

"I can afford it, Howard," he interrupted. "And I want you to have it."

"Thanks," I managed past the lump that had suddenly swelled my throat tight. I stared at the money. "I'll keep in touch. Promise."

"Your mother would like that."

I nodded. His hand came down on my shoulder and gave it an affectionate squeeze. Then Pa stood. I could almost hear the weariness in his body as he straightened and turned back to the house. He paused. I looked up at him, and he at me.

"Whatever you do, Howard, don't forget who your are. What you are. Don't forget what you've learned these seventeen years with us."

He went inside the house.

Chapter Four

Pa went to work the next morning as if the day was no different than any other. I suppose it was his work ethic that he was trying to impress upon me. His one last stab at instilling his set of values. It's not that I had rejected his values. It's just that they weren't mine—exactly. I had nothing against hard work either, so long as it was work I found generally rewarding. Work that I had picked for myself. Not the kind of work Pa picked for me.

At the risk of not showing a good example as far as her work habits were concerned, Ma took the morning off from Deavers' Laundry. Her mothering instincts won out over everything else. She just had to see to it that I had a good lunch, so she packed one in a brown paper sack for me to take along. She hugged me at the top of the steps, and so did Anne and Beth. There were three females there with wet eyes, and I knew mine were soon to follow unless I got out of there quick. My resolve was not all that strong anyway, but I figured that a couple hours down the trail and I'd get to feeling better about what I was doing.

Waldo had found us three horses. I had no idea where he'd come up with them and never asked. They weren't much as far as horseflesh goes, but they each had four legs that worked, and I reckoned that was all I needed to know right then.

I said good-bye to Ma and the girls, and as we rode away from that little frame house where I'd spent so many years I wondered if I would ever see it again. That was all I needed to get the moisture flowing, and I rubbed my eyes, cursing out loud at the wind and the sand. We made our way through Bisbee and out by way of the road that went to Tombstone. I felt better once we were on our way.

All at once Tink threw back his head and let out with a long hoot. "We're finally on our way, Howie!"

I gave a lame grin. "Yeah. No copper mines for us, huh?"

"Nosiree." Tink whipped off his hat and flung it high into the air. It soared across the desert landscape and came to rest in the bright green branches of a paloverde. Tink jabbed his heels and rode off at a gallop, sweeping the hat up and prancing back to Waldo and me. He looked like Menelaus just returned from Troy, with the beautiful Helen riding behind him.

In spite of my heavy spirit, I had to laugh.

Waldo held a tight grin as he looked over his shoulder and scanned the road behind us. "We'll make for Tombstone tonight. Buy you two a couple guns."

"Guns?" Tink asked, settling his hat back onto his head.

"For protection," Waldo said.

Tink looked at me, and I shrugged. "Sure, if you really think that's necessary. But I haven't got any money to buy guns with. Fact is, I haven't got any money at all. Except for five dollars."

"Necessary? Howie, a man ain't hardly outfitted properly in this country unless he's armed."

"I ain't got much either," Tink allowed.

"We'll get some money."

"How?" I asked.

Waldo sent a sly smile my way. "There are ways, Howie."

I wondered what he meant, too green right

then to see what he was driving at. We rode on most of the morning, and as the hours stretched on, Waldo seemed less interested in what was behind him and more excited about what lay ahead.

"Some big happenings took place only a few years back in Tombstone," he said at one point.

I figured he was talking about the famous gunfight at the OK Corral between the Earp bothers and the Clanton gang.

"You two ever been to the Bird Cage Theatre?" he asked.

"Nope," Tink said, "but I've heard of it."

All I knew was that the Bird Cage Theatre was supposed to be sort of like Margot's Palace. A place proper young men did not go to—or so Ma and Pa had warned me. But then, they had said the same thing about the saloons down along Brewery Gulch, and I hadn't seen anything so wrong with them. Looking back, I wondered if they had been giving me the straight of it all along. Brewery Gulch had turned out to be friendly and kinda fun, not the dangerous "slice of hell" that Pa had called it more than once. So maybe Margot's Palace wasn't so bad either. Or the Bird Cage.

"I haven't been either, but I'm game."

Waldo cast an approving look at me that made all my earlier uneasiness melt away. We

51

reached Tombstone midnoon or so, and Waldo said he need a drink. We headed for the nearest watering hole, of which there seemed an endless supply to choose from along Allen Street, and ordered us a couple of beers. Once again, Waldo paid for them, quickly shoving something into his pocket before I had a chance to see.

"Time to make some plans," Waldo said a few minutes later after we'd slaked our thirst and were working our way through our second mug.

"What sorta plans, Waldo?" Tink asked eagerly.

"Money sorta plans," he replied. "I'm nearly broke again. Those horses took almost all of it, and if we are to get you two some guns, well, that's the whole wad."

"I don't see why we need to buy guns to get us a job," I noted.

"Well, that sort of depends on the job, now don't it, Howie?"

I shrugged. "Guess so. What kind of work have you got in mind, Waldo?" A quick glance told me that Tink was curious too. I reckon in all their planning, the two of them had never gotten around to the bricks and mortar of just how they were going to get wealthy, as Waldo had bragged we would.

Waldo cast a quick look around the smoky barroom, then lowered his voice. "You two ever steal anything?" His dark eyes leaped between Tink and me, blazing with a sudden fire.

"No," I said at once.

Tink hesitated. "Well, I guess I took some things that weren't mine." He looked embarrassed and gave me a frown that seemed to be an apology of sorts. "Sorry, Howie. I never told you 'cause I didn't want you to think bad of me."

"I'd never think bad of you, Tink," I replied, uneasy at the direction Waldo had taken this conversation.

"It's easy. We just find out where folks keep their money and then take it."

"I don't know. That's not right." I suddenly heard Preacher Gotlin's hellfire-and-brimstone voice booming out the Ten Commandments inside my head.

"What's not right, Howie? We'll only take from thems what have a lot. They'll hardly miss it. Or do you want to go back to your ma and pa and spend the rest of your days in the mines."

"No," I said, startled by the certainty in my own voice. I'd never done anything that ever went against Pa's beliefs . . . and yet where had his straitlaced living ever gotten him? I shut out Preacher Gotlin's voice. In spite of his warnings, there was a curious tingling vibrating through my body, sorta like the first time I'd ridden a horse full out with the wind tearing off my hat and whipping my hair.

"I didn't think so." Waldo finished his beer. "I think we need something a mite stronger, don't you?"

I looked at Tink, who was looking at me.

Waldo flagged down the barkeep. "Whiskey and three glasses."

He brought a bottle to the table. Waldo pulled a green paisley coin purse from his pocket, and I nearly let out a gasp. But I held it back, and when the bartender had left, Waldo put the purse on the table in front of me and Tink.

"Recognize that?"

"Deaver's! You were the one who broke into the laundry the other night."

"It was like taking candy from a baby. Back door was left unlocked." Waldo filled our glasses and lifted his in sort of a salute. "That's the way it is most times. People just go off leaving a door unlocked or a window opened. They make it easy for clever men like us."

I was shocked, but at the same time the caper intrigued me. Forgetting myself, I snatched up the whiskey and took a drink like it was water. It scorched my throat and surged up into my nose and gagged me as I struggled to keep from coughing it out on Tink or Waldo. My eyes bulged, and Waldo began to laugh. Tink looked on in amazement, concern filling his face. I finally swallowed it all down, and came up for air with a great gasp. I coughed hard and tried to breathe, but my throat had squeezed practically shut. My face was burning, and I imagined my cheeks glowing crimson.

"Take a couple deep breaths," Waldo advised while Tink slapped me on the back and asked if I was all right.

"Course I'm not all right!" I shot back. "Would I be gasping here if I was all right?"

A couple men over at another table were sniggering, and one called over. "Maybe ye ought ta wait till you grow chin whiskers before ye go taking a man's drink."

I'd have melted into the chair if I could have. "That's it," I croaked, my voice sounding funny, my throat raw, "I'm getting outta here."

I heard more laughter as I lurched to my feet and pitched though the batwing doors, starting along the boardwalk.

"Hold up!" Tink called after me, and then he and Waldo were drawing up alongside.

"You got to take whiskey in little sips, Howie," Waldo said.

"Reckon I just must have forgot," I shot back sharply.

"Well, you surely won't forget next time," Tink quipped, grinning.

"Won't be a next time." I adjusted my lopsided hat and dragged a sleeve across my mouth.

"There will be other times," Waldo said with a certainty that drew my eyes around to him. "Like everything else, it takes some learnin'." An easy grin slid across his narrow face like oil on water. It wouldn't be the first time I'd note that tight, self-confident smirk. "There's a general mercantile across the way. Come on."

I slipped a glance Tink's way. "Let's go, Howie. I ain't never owned a gun before."

I reckon if I had anything like "good judgment" left, it was slipping away fast. Like a flood, I was being swept along, and not fighting the currents all that hard. We went into the store and gathered around a glass display box filled with six or seven new revolvers.

"Can I help you boys?" asked a man with a rumbling voice and a beard blacker than the bottom of a coal scuttle. He squeezed himself from behind a counter and came over. He was wearing a smudged apron, and I mused that there was enough material in it to make me a pair of britches, and two shirts to boot.

"Going to buy my friends here a couple guns. Just looking over your wares." Waldo said it like he bought guns every day. Well, it was plain obvious he knew more about the matter than Tink and me together.

"Got some of the best in town." In spite of the booming barrel-bottom voice, the shopkeeper had an easy way about him, and a quick and friendly smile that pushed up his ruddy cheeks and made his small blue eyes glisten. "As you can see, there are some fine Colt's revolvers—the best you can buy. There is a Smith and Wesson if you fancy break-top automatic ejecting firearms. And if you are at the bottom of your pouch, I've got a Forehand and Wadsworth or a Hopkins and Allen for only two-fifty each."

"Hmm." Waldo eyed the Colts, even though the money remaining in Mr. Deaver's filched purse would probably not stretch that far.

"Like them Colts, do you?"

"Nice balance," Waldo replied, patting his own side arm.

"I've got the best prices around. I can beat the Montgomery Wards and Company catalog price by fifty cents."

Waldo's eyebrows hitched up with interest. "What do they fetch?"

"Eleven fifty."

Waldo peeked inside the paisley money pouch and fingered through the coins there. "That the best you can do?"

"You said a couple guns? I'll knock another two bits off the price of each if you buy two."

Waldo counted again, then frowned.

We walked out of there fifteen minutes later with two Forehand and Wadsworth .38s, a pair of holsters, a hundred rounds of cartridges for practicing, and a handful of cheap cigars—all for twelve dollars and sixty cents.

"When we get more money we'll go back for the Colts," Waldo promised as we took to our saddles again and headed out of Tombstone for our first shooting lesson. We collected some bottles along the way and found a place about a quarter mile outside of town where a small hill rose and we could set the bottles up. Waldo twisted them into the rocky soil and stepped off twenty paces. Tink and me, we just stood out of his way until he was ready for us.

He swept back the tail of his frock coat, then stood there like a spring wound up tight as it could go, his right hand hovering near the butt of his Colt. All at once the spring unwound. Waldo's slender hand leaped for the gun, and the next instant it boomed and the bottle shattered. Waldo grinned, twirled the revolver twice, and slipped it neatly back into its oiled holster all in one movement.

"Golly, that's some shootin'," Tink declared.

"With a little practice you can be nearly as

good," Waldo allowed. He bit the end off one of the cigars he'd just bought and put a match to the other end, swelling his skinny chest and blowing a cloud of smoke at the sky. He motioned Tink over. "You give it a try."

There were three bottles standing, and Tink gave them his best dangerous scowl, sorta hunched forward with his hand hovering near the gun as Waldo had done. Then he grabbed for the revolver, fumbled it out of the holster, and dropped it.

Waldo laughed. I grinned too. Tink gave us both an impatient look as he grabbed his gun up and brushed the dirt off it.

"Maybe you should save the draw for later," Waldo advised. "For now, just see if you can break one of those bottles."

"All right." Tink raised the gun and pointed it at the end target.

"It will help if you cock it," Waldo observed casually.

"Oh. Yeah. I forgot." Tink drew back the hammer using both his thumbs, then took a stance, pointed the gun, and pulled the trigger. It barked and leaped in his hand, and a plume of dust erupted about three feet above the bottle.

"Shoots a bit high," Tink said.

"Just a mite," Waldo agreed.

Tink gave it another try. The bullet flew high

again. He emptied the revolver, reloaded, and on his eighth shot nicked the long neck and knocked an inch off the top.

I applauded.

"Pretty good shooting, Wild Bill," Waldo said.

Tink grinned.

"Let Howie have a try at it," Waldo said, and Tink was more than happy to relinquish his position on the firing line.

I stepped up in his place and pointed the gun Waldo had just bought me. I recalled that Tink's first shot went high, so I aimed lower than I thought necessary and fired. The gun kicked up in my hand, and a small puff of dirt rose to the left of the bottle. I gritted my teeth, cocked back the hammer, and took careful aim, using both hands as I'd once seen Deputy Sheriff Frank Gilpin do. My second shot missed too, but not by much more than an inch.

"You're getting the range," Tink encouraged as I got ready for my third go at it. This time I burrowed right under the bottle, toppling it over.

"Next one should do it," Waldo said encouragingly.

I drew a bead on the next bottle over, took my time, caught my breath, and blew it to smithereens. There was a round of applause as if I'd just pitched a no-hitter for the Bisbee Miners.

We practiced until our bullets and targets ran out, and went back into town for a meal. Waldo had just enough money left for the three of us to fill our bellies at a tiny café sandwiched between a barbershop and a confectionery.

"Another couple weeks you two will be handling those hoglegs like a real professional."

"You're pretty good with that six-shooter." Tink's compliment brought a tight smile to Waldo's chiseled face.

"If you want to be good too—"

"I do," Tink said quickly.

"—it's going to take a lot more practice, and that takes lots of bullets, and bullets cost money. Speaking of which, we have reached the bottom of the poke."

I knew where he was going with that, and my stomach curled into a knot, but Tink warmed to the idea.

"You're talking about a holdup?" I asked cautiously.

"Not right away. I say we start small. We'll see who locks their doors and who doesn't. Tonight."

"Where?" I asked quietly, suddenly thinking every ear in the café was turned our way.

"Right here in Tombstone. I always say the best opportunities are usually right where you already are." He grinned.

61

I gave him a lame grin back, wondering what I was letting myself in for, and mighty glad that Pa wasn't around to hear what we were planning.

Chapter Five

We crept through the shadows behind a row of Allen Street buildings that stood off a little way from the saloons, which were still doing a bustling business. Waldo thought we might have better pickings on this end of town. At least these shops were all closed up and dark. But there was still enough noise coming off the street to send a chill up my spine.

A door creaked open ahead, and we flattened into the shadows. I dared not breathe. A shaft of light momentarily lit the alley, then vanished with the closing of the door.

"I don't like this," I said.

"We're all right. Watch where you put your feet."

That was easier said than done, considering

the deep darkness and the junk lying about. Waldo slipped soundlessly from the shadows, looked all around, then tried a nearby window. It was locked. The door to the next building down was locked too. There was an adobe hovel with wooden bars over the windows. We passed it on by. Waldo found an unlocked door, but a chain stopped it from opening more than six inches.

"Damn," he whispered, putting a shoulder to the door and quietly nudging it.

My hands were shaking and my mouth had gone tinder dry. Waldo moved on, testing a window and another door. We were getting awfully close to a saloon whose lights brightened the alleyway enough that I could see a glint of pink off Tink's cheeks.

Tink was moving along the other side of the alley, testing doors, fiddling with windows, bumping noisily in the dark. Just to show that I wasn't completely worthless, I stepped into a darkened doorway and gave the knob a twist. I nearly choked on my own surprise when it clicked over and swung inward.

"Tink! . . . Waldo!" I whispered.

"Good work, Howie," Waldo said, slapping me on the back.

"It—it just opened!" I stammered, but neither of them was listening to me. Waldo quickly stuck his head inside, then slipped out of sight with Tink right behind him. I reluctantly took up the rear, careful to close the door behind me.

"Where are we?" I asked.

"Don't know yet," came Tink's barely whispered reply from the darkness. Ahead, Waldo's footsteps scraped the wooden floor and there was the sound of another door opening. A bit of light from off of Allen Street made its way through the front windows and faintly illuminated Tink as he crept after Waldo.

"It's a drugstore," Waldo announced from ahead. I followed them into the main room. The light here was only marginally better. "Keep away from the windows and your heads down," Waldo warned. "Anyone out on the street who might chance to look this way will see movement if we aren't careful."

A floorboard creaked beneath my feet. There were counters running along each side of the building, and hunkered down behind one of them, I at least felt safe from unwanted eyes. Along the top of the counters were glass display cases. A hinged door at the back of the first one opened easily. I felt around in the dark and recognized the smooth round feel of a watch.

The watch slipped easily—too easily—into my pocket. The next case contained ivory-handled straight razors. Unfortunately, I had no great need of a razor yet. As I moved along, I could hear Tink and Waldo across the shop making their way behind the second counter.

"Find any cash, Howie?" Waldo whispered.

"No."

There was a rustle of a pasteboard carton. A moment later Tink quipped, "Either of you two have need of a bottle of Dr. Kilmer's Female Remedy?"

"Oh yeah, every day," I shot back.

Waldo gave a low chuckle.

The next case held an assortment of spectacles. I didn't have any need for these either. Farther along the counter I came across a display of ear trumpets. I needed an ear trumpet like I needed the spectacles, but I stuck one against my ear anyway and aimed it toward the other side of the building where I could hear Tink and Waldo rustling a bit louder.

"Ooh! Lookie what I found," Waldo said with a note of delight.

"What?" Tink asked softly.

"I'll show you later, when we get out of here."

I wasn't having much luck on my side of the shop. I returned the ear trumpet to its place and turned around and headed back the way I came.

The sound of a drawer being opened was followed by Tink's excited voice. "Here's the cash, Waldo."

Now that they had found what they were after, I figured we'd be leaving. I was anxious to be out of there, and I started around the counter toward the rear door. I'd no sooner got into the open than a shadow darkened the window and moved across the floor and me. A man had stopped on the sidewalk and was peering inside. I froze, my heart delivering sledgehammer blows to my rib cage. With my face bent toward the window, I knew the light was hitting it. He just stood there a moment as if looking for something on the dark shelves, his tall form a silhouette against the light from a saloon across the street. In the grips of a panic, I suddenly pulled back behind the counter. His head shot around at that moment, and I knew I'd given us away.

"I've been seen!" I whispered.

"Don't move," Waldo's soft command was emphatic.

"We've got to get out of here!" Panic rose in my voice, and I fought to control it.

"Howie, get a grip," Tink said. "I can see him. He's not sure. He's not doing a thing. He's just looking now."

The man's shadow shifted across the floor as if he was seeking a different angle to view the darkened interior. I didn't breathe—*couldn't* breathe as I lay there, pressing hard against the counter.

A minute ticked by, then two, and then the shadow moved off.

"He's going," Tink said.

"I'm outta here!" I scrambled to my feet and dashed through the connecting door. In the dark room I tripped on a box, knocked something over with my elbow, then bumped into the closed alley door. Grappling at the handle, I flung it open and leaped outside.

"Here, what's this?" a voice slurred, surprised. Two men standing in the back door of a saloon across the way had come about and were staring at me. It was impossible for them to see who I was in the dark alley. Just the same, I wheeled away in a panic and flew off in the opposite direction.

Tink and Waldo emerged next.

"Hey, you two!" The men lurched out of the doorway, and Tink and Waldo scattered in different directions.

They were out of there, and that was all that mattered to me. I lowered my head, put on a burst of speed.

We made camp a few miles out of town and lay low most of the next day. But I could see that Waldo was anxious about something, so about four o'clock we saddled our horses and rode back into Tombstone. He said he was hungry, so we found a run-down hash shack near Boot Hill and ordered the special of the day, fried liver and onions, with fried potatoes and boiled peas.

Waldo ate distractedly, keeping one eye cocked toward the window. I figured he was on the lookout for the law, but then suddenly he jumped up and hurried out the door. He came back a minute later unfolding a copy of the *Tombstone Epitaph*, forgot his food, and began eagerly rustling the pages.

"What're you looking for?" Tink asked, scraping peas onto his fork with a knife.

"News of the robbery," he said, impatiently turning pages.

"No news is good news, far as I'm concerned," I said.

Waldo was scowling. "You'd think there would be something—" Suddenly he stopped and glared at the paper. "What's this?

Petty thieves broke into the Kroger Drug Store late last night. They made off with a few dollars in change and knocked over a clothes tree on the way out. Jim Spline and Walter Kapshaw spied the robbers fleeing down the alley at about midnight and claim they looked to be kids out for a lark. Herrmann Kroger says he is planning to install a heavier lock on his back door.

"Petty thieves! Kids out for a lark! Can you believe it? A heavier lock? It would help if he used the one he already had!"

I didn't see what had upset Waldo so, but he was sulky all the rest of the day until we got back to camp. We'd bought two boxes of .38 cartridges, and he commenced to getting Tink and me to practice some more with our new guns.

We popped bottles until dark and then settled down around the campfire. Waldo had smoked the last of his cigars, and now he fished a cardboard box out of his pocket and extracted a thin cigarette. "Ever try one of these?"

"Cigarette?" Tink nodded. "Sure, I've smoked 'em plenty of times."

"Not just a cigarette," Waldo corrected, "and I'll bet you never smoked one like this. It's one of them cocaine cigarettes the Parke-Davis Company makes."

"Where'd you get 'em?" I asked.

"I found them in the drugstore last night. Here, try one." Waldo passed the box around. Our curiosity had been hard scratched, so we each took one. It tasted pretty much like any other cigarette except there was an extra bite to it that seemed to linger in my throat, as if the smoke was hotter than usual. There was a strange odor about them, too.

Tink gave a hoot and a laugh and said, "Like smoking a doggone dragon."

"Easier going down than that whiskey," I noted.

"It gets even easier—just wait."

As usual, Waldo was right. After a few minutes, I didn't feel the smoke at all. My spirits were suddenly soaring, and I had forgotten all about what had gotten me down earlier. All I knew was that I felt fine. If there'd been another drugstore to rob, I was right ready to do the job.

Waldo drew his gun and began shooting branches off a nearby fallen tree, while Tink pranced along its trunk doing his famous impersonation of a chicken with its head cut off, pretending to be skipping over the bullets. I laughed until my eyes teared, and then I laughed some more.

Later, light-headed and dreamy, we sat around the campfire making plans for our lives—as if a seventeen-year-old and two eighteen-year-old kids knew enough to plan out their entire lives in one evening.

Waldo had aspirations of bigger and grander capers. Tink only wanted to get some money in his pocket and find himself a good town somewhere to hunker down in. Me, I wanted to see the world, but that took lots of money. When I told them so, Waldo said, "Stick with me, Howie, and you'll have all the money you'll need."

It must have been those crazy cigarettes doing my thinking for me right then, because I said I would, and asked what our next larceny was going to be.

Waldo had already figured that out.

We headed north, robbed a grocery store in Sulphur Springs and a mining supply store in Dos Cabezas, then bent our trail west and broke into a freight depot in Casa Grande. We swung south again and stole a couple guns from a hardware store in Tucson. I figured we were doing all right for ourselves in our new career, but something had started to bother Waldo. He'd become more and more withdrawn and sulky, and whenever he got like that Tink and I gave him a wide berth, not certain what it all meant.

We lay low for a while in the Rincon Mountains, camped along a cool stream where Waldo furthered our education in the proper use of the new Colts we had stolen. The guns were .45s, and they bucked harder than the .38s we'd bought back in Tombstone, but they had a nice feel and were easy to use. "Point-and-shoot

guns" is what Waldo liked to call them, and
once Tink and I got to where we could bust bottles almost as well as Waldo, he began to show
us some of his little tricks that would give us an
advantage in a gunfight. It was not like we'd had
to use our guns for anything except busting bottles so far, but Waldo felt certain the time would
come.

"There's something you got to keep in mind,"
Waldo said once after we'd spent an hour or so
practicing drawing our guns and shooting at
pinecones scattered out across the ground.
"Sometimes you aren't going to be able to get
an advantage like the sun behind your back, or
shooting from higher ground. Sometimes
you've got to make an advantage right where
you are at."

"Yeah, like hauling a brick wall along to shoot
from behind," Tink said, and chuckled.

I grinned. Tink was always clowning. Even
when the day was gloomy, Tink could find a ray
of sunshine poking through the clouds somewhere.

Waldo rolled his eyes. Sometimes he got impatient with Tink's funning around, but this
time he gave a short, soundless laugh. Waldo's
mood had improved over the days, and it always was rosiest when we were out with our
guns, popping bottles or tin cans.

"You can haul a brick wall around with you if that's what you want," Waldo said. "I prefer something a little lighter. Something a mite more elegant."

"Elegant?" I asked. "Like what?"

Waldo pulled out one of the cigars he always kept in an inside pocket and rolled it in his fingers.

"I'll take a brick wall any day," Tink said.

"How's that supposed to help?" I pressed.

"It is called distraction. You want to put your enemy off his guard. Getting him to lower it just a bit is all the advantage you need sometimes."

"You gonna offer it to him, or just stand there waving it in front of his nose?"

"Neither. I'm going to smoke it." Waldo bit the end off and put it between his lips. His left hand dipped into a pocket and came out with a match. His thumbnail scratched it to life. Fire flared, naturally catching my eye, and in that instant Waldo's right hand swept down and snapped the revolver from its holster. It came up lightning quick, cocked and ready to fire, and pointed right at my chest.

"Bang," he said softly.

I swallowed hard to force the lump back down my throat. He elevated the muzzle and gently lowered the hammer. "Distraction," he said with a quiet intensity. "It can be one of your best allies. Figure out a couple of your own and then don't forget them when the time comes."

"When are we ever going to need to know that?" Tink bent for one of the spent cartridge shells and turned it toward the sun, watching the light slide along the bright brass curve.

"Soon."

Tink looked up. "What does that mean?"

"It means I'm getting tired of sneaking around in the dark hoping someone has left a door unlocked. It means it's about time we start to make a reputation for ourselves."

"Reputation?" I asked. "I don't want a reputation. What's wrong with sneaking around in the dark? We've gotten pretty good at picking locks, you know."

"We'll never get anywhere picking locks, Howie. Where would Jesse James have been without a reputation? Or Billy the Kid, or John Wesley Hardin, or Charles Bolton?"

"Alive?" Tink suggested.

Waldo gave a quick scowl. "That's not what I mean."

"So, what do you mean? What do we have to do to get a reputation?" Waldo had something on his mind, something that had been chewing at him for days, and I wanted to know what it was.

His dark eyes brightened, the fire of adventure and excitement burning suddenly in them. "First thing we got to do is get us a name. Then we got to make people aware of it."

"How do you do that?" Tink asked.

"By not scurrying around in the night like pack rats, collecting the castoffs people leave behind."

Tink gave me a worried look, then shifted it toward Waldo. "Are you saying you want to hold up a store in the daylight?"

"Sure! But not just stores anymore. We'll hold up trains, and banks, and payroll shipments."

"You're crazy," I said.

"Why? That's what Jesse James did."

"And he's dead!" I pointed out to him again, just in case he had forgotten what Tink had said.

But Waldo didn't appear to be listening to me. "How 'bout the Fritz Gang?"

"The Fritz Gang?" I shook my head. "How about we just forget this foolhardy notion. You're going to get us all killed."

Waldo still wasn't listening.

Chapter Six

A hot wind shoved a swirl of dust drunkenly down the middle of the main street of Oro Blanco. I was feeling the heat more than usual as I stood on the boardwalk out front of Hoiser's Family Grocers across the street from the Oro Blanco Miner's Union Bank. I tried to look inconspicuous, but felt certain every passerby was giving me the eye and wondering what I was up to. There were a lot of people out and about.

Waldo had stationed me there to keep an eye out for the law while he and Tink went across the street to give the bank a closer look. They'd been in there a long time, I thought, dragging my sweaty palms on the canvas vest I'd stolen in Arivaca a month or two back. I took out my watch—at least I considered it mine, as I did everything else we'd stolen. Only five minutes had passed. Then all at once Waldo and Tink stepped out the door and angled across the street. Tink gave me a nod to follow.

"An armed guard near the door and the place is packed like sardines in a can," Tink said as we stood beneath a shady cottonwood tree out behind the livery at the edge of town.

"Just too many people in there," Waldo agreed, disappointed.

"Must be payday at the mines," I suggested. "The town is full of people. Well, maybe another day." I tried to sound disappointed.

"We can't wait another day," Waldo shot back. "We're flat out of money, in case you haven't noticed."

"My stomach has been wondering about that," Tink said, giving Waldo a lopsided grin.

Waldo ignored him, his scowl deepening. "I'm not leaving here until we get some money." His hard stare fell upon me. "See any lawmen about town?"

"No. None that I noticed, anyway."

"Well, that's something." His heavy eyebrows hooded his narrowed eyes as he considered our next move.

Tink was glancing around Oro Blanco as if he was pondering something too. "This looks like it might be a good town," he mumbled to himself, then saw me staring and grinned. "Just wondering, that's all."

"It's a mining town, Tink," I reminded him.

He grimaced, then shook his head. "You're right. Not a good town."

"All right, this is what we are going to do," Waldo said suddenly. He lowered his voice, even though we were alone and no one else was nearby to hear. "We'll find a shop that's not busy. We'll bust in there with our guns drawn and demand the cash box. What do you think?"

"I think we're asking for trouble with all these people in town."

He scowled at me. "You're scared, that's all."

"I am not," I said too quickly.

Tink said, "What will we do if they don't give us the cash box?"

"Yeah, then what?"

Waldo considered, some of that earlier fire flickering now before a new wind of uncertainty.

"We ain't going to shoot anyone," I went on.

It was the first time I'd ever seen Waldo fumble for an answer. "Then . . . then we'll leave, and try some other town."

"That will build us some kind of reputation, won't it." Tink swept his arm in a grand, dramatic arc. "I can see the headlines now. 'Fritz

79

Gang Run Out of Oro Blanco by Tough-Talking Shopkeeper!' " He laughed. "Better just hope the proprietor isn't a proprietess."

"Go on, have your joke." Waldo endured Tink's mirth until Tink had finally gone quiet, then he said, "Let's go find us somebody to rob."

We trailed after Waldo, collected our horses, and began walking them down the street, eyeing each business as we strolled past.

The milliner's shop was full of women, the hardware store full of men. The baker and three grocers were busy too. We'd already ruled out the bank, and while we were eyeing a drugstore, a man wearing a badge came along and turned into its door.

Waldo let out a soft curse, and we moved on.

There was a meat market, but the proprietor looked the sort of man who might slaughter his beef barehanded, so we moved on. A real estate agent looked promising. When we tried the door, it was locked and no one was inside. We agreed to avoid the attorney at law, considered the dry goods store, but backed off when a little lady stuck her head out the door of the specialty dress shop next door and waved pleasantly at us.

"She saw our faces," Waldo mumbled under his breath as we moved on. We stepped into a saloon to think this over. We each itched for a beer, but there was no money yet to pay for even one.

"Come on," Waldo said disgustedly, resuming our quest. Then we saw it. We all three stopped at once, as if the same thought had struck us like a single bolt of lightning. We were standing in front of a barbershop, peering through the plate glass at three absolutely empty chairs and two bored barbers reading the newspaper.

Waldo said quickly, "This is what we'll do. Tink, you stay near the door. Howie, you come with me. You keep 'em covered while I get the cash box. Got it?"

I got it, but only in a vague sort of way, because my brain was suddenly reeling with excitement and fear. It happened so quickly, I hardly had time to grasp what it was we were about to do. All I remember was sidling up to the doorway, casting one last glance up and down the sidewalk, then pulling our bandannas up over our noses and turning into that barbershop.

"Hands in the air," Waldo ordered, pointing his gun as we barged on through the doorway.

The barbers' newspapers rustled to the floor and their hands shot for the ceiling. I blinked sweat from my eyes as I followed Waldo inside and held my gun on them, trying to keep my hand from shaking.

"What's this about?" one of them asked, as if he couldn't tell by our masks and guns that we were sticking the place up. Out the corner of my eye, Tink moved into place by the door and just stood there. Both barbers were eyeing us nervously.

Before Waldo could answer the gent's obvious question, the second fellow, a middle-aged man with oiled, slicked-back salt-and-pepper hair and a sharply trimmed mustache, said, "Cash is in a box inside that cabinet, mister."

Waldo tried the door. It was locked.

"Where's the key?"

"Right here, around my neck." He cautiously rotated one hand and pointed a finger downward.

"Get over here and open it," Waldo ordered.

"I will, mister. Just don't shoot." The barber got off the chair and removed the key, which was held by a thong. I stepped around one of the chairs to keep an eye on him and the other barber, a younger man whose face had suddenly emptied of all color. My head was beginning to clear, and I was growing more confident as the seconds ticked by. I cast a nervous glance at Tink. He was still guarding the door, and so far no one had come in for a shave or a cut.

The older barber unlocked the cabinet door and reached inside, but Waldo stopped him.

"That's good enough. Just back away some." He reached inside the cabinet. "I thought so." Waldo's voice carried a sneer with it, and I saw that he was holding a little revolver. "That kinda stunt will get you killed, mister," Waldo growled.

"I wasn't going to use it," the barber said, and he was being real calm about it as he stepped up alongside the chair near where I was standing. "The gun was atop the box, that's all."

Waldo retrieved a metal box and shook it. The distinctive rattle of coins inside was a reassuring sound.

"Let's get," Tink said suddenly. "Looks like someone's coming this way."

Waldo glanced over at Tink, then back at the man. "Just so you know, you've been held up by the Fritz Gang," he said, and he started for the door. But before I had taken a step, that barber grabbed ahold of the stropping leather hanging off the chair and swung it out. It slapped my hand with a serpent's bite, and my gun clattered to the floor. Before I could move, the barber was diving for it.

"Waldo!" I cried.

It all happened in a blur of motion; the next instant Waldo was at my side, swinging the revolver in his hand. The barrel cracked down alongside the barber's head with a thump, then the man's unconscious body was at my feet and someone was tugging me toward the door. I remembered the sunlight glaring in my eyes, and then somehow I was back atop my horse and hightailing it out of there.

"Sorry, Waldo. Guess I must have took my eyes off of him for a second."

"Sorry! You almost got us all killed, Howie!"

"Aw, lay off him, Waldo," Tink called down at him for maybe the third or fourth time. We were well hidden back up a hot and dry and dusty ravine about five or six miles from town. Tink had scampered up one of the loose, steep sides to a rock that looked out past the mouth of the ravine to where the trail snaked away.

Waldo scowled at me, then stomped over to his horse and pulled the cash box out of his saddlebag where he had wedged it tight.

"Anyway, we got out of there all right, didn't we?" I hoped pointing out some positive things might help cool him down some. Waldo had been burning under the collar. We'd just managed to escape Oro Blanco by the skin of our teeth.

"No thanks to you." He set the box on a rock and fooled with the latch. It was locked. "Damn!" Grabbing up a melon-size boulder,

Waldo flung it onto the steel box, bursting it open.

Tink clambered off the rock, sliding down the crumbly slope and brushing the dust from the seat of his britches as he came over. "There ain't nobody coming." He drew up and peered down at the few coins scattered across the dirt. When he saw the startled look on Waldo's face, he added, "What could you expect? They weren't exactly doing a booming business when we went in there."

Waldo collected the money and counted it up. "All that trouble for this?" he snarled. "You nearly got us all thrown in jail for a few dollars!"

I stared at the nickels and quarters in his fist. "I . . . I just lost my head," I mumbled contritely.

"That isn't all you lost," he shot back, glaring at the empty holster around my waist in a way that made me wish there were a hole to crawl into. "That Colt was worth about twelve dollars, and this cash box held seven dollars and thirty-seven cents. The way I figure it, our first-ever daylight robbery has just cost us four dollars and sixty-three cents, thanks to you, Howie."

"Aw, lay off him, Waldo," Tink warned again. "Least we got away with a little money—enough to buy some food."

Waldo wheeled back around toward me.

"You're just lucky I was there to help you, Howie, or you'd probably be dead now, or locked up in a jail cell. You owe me one."

I was feeling plain awful, and I didn't think Waldo was in any mood for me to point out that it was his doings in the first place that had us in that barbershop trying to pull off a foolhardy daylight robbery. I didn't say anything.

Tink stepped between Waldo and me. "All right, I mean it now. Lay off of him, Waldo, or we both ride out of here."

I rarely ever heard Tink get mad. He was more likely to make a joke than a threat, but he was mighty close to mad now.

Waldo saw it too and let go of his anger. "Okay. I won't say no more about it." He grabbed up the box, dumped the money back into it, and strode back to his horse.

Tink put a hand on my shoulder. "It's all right, Howie. This sort of thing, it's all new to us. You couldn't help it."

"Thanks," I said quietly.

"Looking out for you is my job in life." He gave me one of his big smiles, and suddenly I was feeling a little better.

We rode on to Calabasa that afternoon and had ourselves a good dinner at a little adobe café, then bought some supplies, including a box of

.38s for my old Forehand and Wadsworth revolver that I resurrected out of my saddlebags.
It filled the empty place in my holster, but I sure
missed that Colt. I had gotten to the point where
I could shoot passably straight with it.

As the day faded toward night, Waldo perked
up some more, and finally he seemed to have
let go of the rest of his disappointment over the
botched robbery, and me. We built a fire and
rolled out our beds, and he offered us each one
of the cocaine cigarettes that he'd bought back
in Calabasa. But neither Tink nor I much cared
for them. They sure made you believe you could
whip the world when you were smoking them,
but then afterward, when they wore off, there
was always a crushing wave of discontentment.
Lately, Waldo seemed to be craving them more
than ever, and his mood definitely improved
once he got one.

I was feeling homesick and wondered why. I
thought I had gotten over that months ago, but
suddenly I was thinking of Ma and Pa—especially Pa—and feeling a pang. I knew why, but
I refused to let my brain ponder it.

"Well, boys, hate to break it to you again, but
you know that seven dollars and thirty-seven
cents we got this morning? Well, it's all gone but
about four bits."

I knew what that meant, and so did Tink. "So, what's next, Waldo?" Tink asked.

"There are a couple towns to the north of us along this here road. There's Hartins, and Saunders, and Casa Blanca, that I know of."

"This road goes to Tombstone, don't it?" Tink asked.

"It does, but I don't expect that we need to go that far before coming across some isolated store. There're lots of 'em around here, keeping the miners stocked up with supplies. I figure we'll just find us a store that ain't too close to any town and do what we do best."

"Holdups?" Tink asked, a smirk in his voice. "Oh, great, the fearsome Fritz Gang strikes again."

"All right. So we had us some trouble today," Waldo went on, refusing to succumb to our malaise. "We'll do better next time. It's all a matter of learning the ropes."

"We had a lot better luck just breaking into places at night," I pointed out.

"Yeah, but we weren't building a reputation."

"And you like the reputation we've built so far?" Tink asked.

Waldo frowned.

"Who needs a reputation, anyway?" I grumped.

"I do!" Waldo snapped. He drew long and

heavy on his cigarette, then turned on his heels and walked out of the firelight into the night.

Tink rubbed his chin. "That man sure is a driven sonuva—" he started to say, then stopped, compressed his eyes in sudden concentration, and rubbed his chin some more. "Howie, take a looky here. What daya see?"

"Bend closer to the fire."

He did.

"Looks to me like you've got yourself the start of a decent beard."

"Shoot-howdy! The devil you say?"

"Cross my heart."

Tink grinned, and stroked the darkening fuzz some more. "Wish I had me a mirror."

"Steal yourself one tomorrow."

"Just might do that. Yessiree, I just might do that!"

"You got any paper?" I asked.

He peered hopefully into a pot of water. But it was too dark to give back any kind of reflection. "Paper? No, why?"

"Thought I'd write Ma and Pa and the girls a letter."

"That's a good idea. I ought to write my folks too. We'll steal that tomorrow too."

"Yeah." I tossed out the coffee at the bottom of my cup and left Tink by the fire, feeling his face.

The nights had taken on a chill here lately, and that meant fall was coming on. The stars looked cold and distant, and the sudden yap of a coyote only added to my already heavy heart.

I wasn't near as easy about what we were doing as Tink appeared to be. He and Waldo seemed to be enjoying this life, while all I really wanted to do was go back home. I wondered what was happening in Bisbee, and wished I knew how my family was faring. Maybe life as a miner wouldn't have been as bad as I had imagined. It had to beat what I was doing now. One thing for sure, I couldn't be a much worse miner than I was a robber! Others had taken to my pa's way of life and seemed happy enough. What was wrong with me?

I kicked at a stone, then strolled back into camp. Waldo had returned and was sitting by the fire. In the flickering light he was taking down his revolver and rubbing each of the pieces with a rag.

I strolled over to my groundsheet, bunched my saddlebags into a pillow, rolled up in my blanket, and went to sleep.

Chapter Seven

We spent the winter robbing general stores, boot makers, saddle makers, a real estate office, even a town marshal's office one bold night. Most of our jobs were pulled off after dark, as we seemed better fit to this sort of work. But Waldo kept insisting on the occasional daylight robbery. Waldo had a flare for the dramatic, and he was determined to build a reputation for himself and Tink and me. So at least once a month the Fritz Gang would strike—usually a lonely outpost where the owner valued his life more than his cash box. Not that anyone's life had ever been in any serious jeopardy from the Fritz Gang. We weren't out to kill no one. Just take their money.

The month of April had gone by without a

strike from the notorious Fritz Gang, whose name had yet to turn up in any newspaper, to Waldo's deep consternation. It was time to make another appearance, and that is how we found ourselves one spring morning on a hill overlooking the rutted track of a lonely road whereupon sat a sun-bleached and weather-worn general mercantile store. I reckoned that the proprietor of that store must have hailed from Bisbee, judging by the lack of paint on the bare boards.

"Perfect," Waldo declared. "It's isolated, and by the looks of it, there doesn't appear to be another soul around."

Butterflies had returned to my belly, but I was determined not to foul up in some stupid way as I had so often in the past. I wanted to make both Tink and Waldo proud of me. "It'll be easy."

Waldo grinned. "A piece of cake."

"Oh, yeah?" Tink piped up. "Look there. Someone is about to take a big bite out of your cake, Waldo." He pointed at four riders who had just rounded a bend in the road.

They cantered up to the store and dismounted, wrapping their reins about the hitching rail. They were too far off to make out clearly, but one thing I was sure of, they didn't have the look of miners. I knew miners well enough to spot the signs a mile off.

"Now what?" I asked, disappointment showing, for in spite of my misgivings, I was anxious to prove myself to my friends.

Tink watched Waldo for a reply, all the while pulling at the short hairs on his chin and cheeks that had blossomed over the winter into a fairly decent beard.

Waldo thought it over while below us the men gathered in front of the store. They spoke briefly among themselves, then moved inside.

Waldo's jaw took a firm set and his dark eyes narrowed against the morning sunlight that drew out all the sharp, angular planes of his thin face. "Nothing changes. All this means is that there are four more sets of pockets to rob. Come on." He urged his horse down the slope. Tink and me, we shared a concerned look, then followed along behind him.

Drawing up behind the store, we quietly dismounted and adjusted our bandannas to hide our faces. Waldo started along the shadow side of the building toward the front. At the corner he gave the road a final glance. Then with a nod we made for the doorway.

I was worried more riders would show up. My gun was in my hand and ready, while my heart began doing the cancan inside my chest.

Just as we burst inside, a gunshot exploded within the building. Startled, we came to a halt, and at the same time the four men wheeled about. Their guns were drawn and their faces covered like ours. We all stood there for an instant, staring at each other. An older man in a dingy apron was lying on the floor, a pool of red slowly seeping from beneath him.

"You killed him," I croaked.

"Get 'em, boys!" one of the men shouted, and the next moment gunfire and smoke filled the store. I can't remember much of what happened next except that somehow I found myself on the floor and behind a counter. A shape rushed past that I knew wasn't Waldo's or Tink's, so I fired and saw it stagger half a step. Bottles were shattering, glass raining down. Men shouted, bullets ripped the wood all around me. Someone crashed through a display, scattering cans of condensed soup all across the floor. I fired at another shape, then covered my head and curled into the tightest ball I could.

The deafening roar of gunfire continued on for what seemed like ages, although I suspect, thinking back on it, that the whole affair couldn't have lasted more than thirty seconds.

And as suddenly as it had started, it was over. The room was suddenly deadly quiet, except for the tinkle of glass still falling and a *glug, glug,*

glug from some overturned barrel of water, or oil or . . . I sniffed, pickles!

Unfolding myself, I cautiously lifted an eye above the counter. My bandanna was down around my neck again, but that didn't seem important right then.

"Waldo? Tink?" I whispered.

"You all right, Howie?" Tink's voice sounded from across the way.

"Yeah. Think so."

There was a rustle of paper and the clatter of cans, and suddenly Waldo's face appeared around a fifty-pound sack of corn meal, leaking from three or four bullet holes.

"What happened?" I said, for as yet my brain hadn't put all the pieces together.

"We busted in on another gang in the middle of robbing this place," Waldo said, standing and brushing the meal from his clothes.

"Gol-dang, what a wreck!" Tink emerged from his hiding place, looking around.

It was hard to believe seven men could have done so much damage in such a short time. "Anyone hit?" I asked worriedly.

"No."

"No."

I went to the door and cautiously looked outside. The horses were gone, but there was lots of blood on the ground. "They're gone. A couple of 'em were bleeding pretty bad." The reality of what had just happened was beginning to sink in, and I began to shake.

Tink bent over the man on the floor. "He's dead."

"This could mean big trouble for us, boys," Waldo said, his dark view shifting around the ruined store. "We better get out of here before someone comes along."

Just then something scraped the floor. We all heard it and turned at once. There was something else, too: a low, strangled whimper, like someone was trying to hold back a sneeze. Waldo's hand leaped for his gun, but I waved him back. I knew that sound. I'd heard it once before, a couple years back when our dog Rex had showed up on the doorstep, bleeding from a gunshot to its chest. Afterward, Beth had disappeared out behind the privy. I had found her curled against the wall, her knees drawn up tight in her small arms, whimpering and trying not to burst out in a full-blown cry.

The sound was coming from behind one of the counters, and somehow I knew what I would find back here. Curled up in a corner was a little girl with long black hair, wearing a green dress and white apron. She couldn't have been much older than eleven or twelve. Her wide, watery eyes fixed upon me when I came around, and she tried to scoot farther back into the corner, but she was already as tight as a body could get.

"I'm not going to hurt you," I said gently, slowly dropping to my haunches.

The stretched, frightened eyes fixed upon my face.

"Are you all right? You aren't hurt, are you?" I heard Tink and Waldo come up behind me. "These are my friends."

She just stared.

"What's your name?" I asked.

But all I got were those big brown eyes, riveted as if seeing the devil himself. I tried a different tack.

"Those men who did this, they're gone. We run them out of here."

Her eyes shifted. I'd made inroads. "I want to help you. Tell me your name."

A blink and a swallow, and then softly, "Alice."

"My name is Howie, and this is Waldo and Tink."

Her view went past me, then came back.

"It's all over," I said, and extended a hand to her. "Come with me. You're safe now."

She hesitated, then reached up and folded her small soft hand into my own rough hands. I helped her out of her cramped corner and started her toward the door. But she stopped stiff as a snubbing post when she saw the man on the floor.

"Don't look at that," Waldo said, gently turning Alice away.

"Come on," Tink said. "You need to get out of here."

We brought Alice outside and sat her on a bench there.

"What about my grandpa?" she asked, her lip quivering.

I shook my head.

Her eyes began to fill again.

"Do you know who those men were?" Waldo asked.

"No. They just came in with guns. My grandpa . . ." The word caught in her throat. "He pushed me behind the penny sweets counter and then . . . and then . . ." She couldn't continue and began to sob openly. I figured that was a good thing, letting it all out as she was doing.

"What are we going to do?" Tink asked.

We both looked to Waldo, who always seemed to know what we should be doing next.

"I don't know," Waldo said. "We should be getting out of here." He was looking nervous.

"We can't leave Alice here by herself," I said.

"No, no, I suppose not," Waldo agreed, but I

could tell he wasn't sure what we ought to be doing.

"I think we ought to go for a sheriff or someone," Tink said.

"We can't do that!" Waldo shot back, keeping his voice down to a whisper.

I said to Alice, "Do you have family nearby? Someone we could take you to?"

She shook her head.

"Nobody?" Tink pressed.

Alice sniffed, and swept the tears from her eyes with a finger. "I got an uncle in Elfrida."

"We can take you there," I said.

Waldo suddenly stiffened and turned, staring up the road. Three men came into view, riding like they had urgent business somewhere . . . here! They drew up around us and took one look at little Alice's red eyes and gave us each a hard, nail-driving glare.

"What happened here?" one of the men asked, his view stuck on Alice.

I scrambled to think of an answer, but before I could come up with one, Waldo spoke up.

"This place has just been held up, mister. A man inside there is dead. Me and my friends had just tied our horses in the shade out back when we heard gunfire from inside. We come in on them having just killed the owner and

about to rob the place. Shot it out and they run
off."

Well, that wasn't exactly the way of it, but I
did admire Waldo's quick thinking, and the way
he twisted the story around just enough to keep
us out of the frying pan . . . I hoped.

The spokesman motioned to one of the men,
who hopped off his horse and went inside. "Is
that the way it happened, Alice?" he asked.

The little girl nodded her head, scrubbing
fresh tears from her eyes.

He eased up some then and said to us, "One
of 'em ended up alongside the road about a
quarter mile from here. Bled to death before we
could get out of him what had happened."

"I wounded one," I admitted.

"Well, you did more than just wound him,
son. You killed him dead as a brass tack. Seems
you three boys come along just in time."

Dead! My head swam, and I felt vaguely ill. I
had a sudden image in my brain of a man bleeding out his life into the dusty road because of
me. I forced the vision out of my head and
grabbed for the rim of a flour barrel to steady
myself as the fellow went on, apparently not no-
ticing my distress.

"It was fortunate for little Alice here that we
did," Waldo went on, seeing an advantage and
seizing it.

"You from around these parts?"

"Douglas—Bisbee," Waldo and I said at the same time.

He studied us and said, "Which is it?"

Tink grinned. "Waldo here, he's from Douglas. Me and Howie, we come from Bisbee."

The man emerged from the store. "Old man Haynes is dead. The place is pretty much shot to pieces. It appears these fellows showed up in time to stop the robbery."

"But too late to save the old man," Waldo said, deep regret in his voice as he dolefully shook his head. "Sorry about that."

"Well, you did what you could," the spokesman allowed. "I reckon we need to get Sheriff Hackler out here to take care of this matter."

Waldo and Tink exchanged worried looks. But me, I didn't see any reason to fear waiting for the sheriff, considering the poor impression the Fritz Gang had left on the folks in this part of the Arizona Territory. I figured at times like this, Waldo should be glad our names had never appeared in any of the newspapers we'd ever seen.

Sheriff Pat Hackler arrived about an hour later with a couple of deputies and a freight wagon to haul the body away in. He was a fat man who needed a shave and smelled like a Brewery Gulch saloon. He gave the place a quick glance-over, and after they had loaded Haynes into the wagon he thanked us for our help. I felt sorta proud for a moment, until I remembered that we had been there to do what those criminals had failed to—with the exception of killing anyone, of course. We'd agreed early on that if it came to gunplay we'd back down gracefully if we could. It was only in preparation for those times when we couldn't back down that Waldo kept schooling us in the use of our guns.

"Don't reckon I need to detain you boys any longer," Hackler said as he and his deputies mounted up. "Far as I know, old Franklin Haynes didn't have any other kin." He studied the store. "Reckon I'll get some men to board the place up in the event someone comes along to claim it." His view shifted lazily toward Alice. "Sorry Alice. Know this is real hard on you. I'll see if I can't find someone who needs help around their place to take you in."

"She has family in Elfrida," I said, placing a hand on the little girl's shoulder. "We'll take her there, and we'll tell the family what happened here. They'll probably come out to take care of this business."

"Howie," Waldo hissed under his breath, but near enough for me to hear.

I ignored him. I was thinking of Anne and

Beth right then. If this had happened to them, I would want someone to step in and help—to seek out a relative, not just drop them off with anyone who happened to be looking for extra hands to help with the cooking and scrubbing and mending.

Pat Hackler nodded his head, apparently relieved to be out from under the job of finding a place for Alice to stay. "That is right decent of you three." He shifted his mouth to one side as if giving it some thought, but I knew he'd made up his mind right from the start. "How does that sit with you, little Alice? You want these three gents to take you to your kin in Elfrida?"

The poor girl was still in a state of shock, but she managed to nod her head and say she did.

"Reckon that settles it, then. I'll have this place closed up and boarded over and I'll wait to hear from the family." He scrubbed the stubble on his chin. "Not much more any of us can do around here. You three take care of little Alice."

"We will," I promised. "Got a sister not much older than Alice back in Bisbee." I don't know why I added that. I got the impression Hackler was relieved to be free of the responsibility of Alice and would have let Jesse James and his gang take her away if it meant he didn't have to deal with the problem.

Hackler, his deputies, and the wagon started up the road. Waldo gave me a narrow stare that I ignored.

"Come on," I said. "Elfrida is a long ride from here."

"Particularly so," commented Waldo unhappily, "since we still ain't got no money."

Tink and I went around back to our horses. When Waldo showed up a few minutes later he was smiling, and I reckoned we now had some spending cash.

"You didn't," I said.

"The old man would have wanted it so," Waldo said under his breath. "Wouldn't want his granddaughter to go hungry, now, would he?"

I frowned and climbed into my saddle. I gave Alice a hand up onto my bedroll behind me and waited until she had squirmed herself into place and had arranged her skirt to cover her ankles. Finally she threaded her small arms about my waist and we got moving.

"Your uncle have a name?" Tink asked as we started onto the road.

"His name is Uncle Ed."

"Has Uncle Ed got a last name?" Waldo asked.

"Berger," she replied.

"I've never been to Elfrida," Tink said. "Have any of you?"

Both Waldo and I shook our heads.

"Does it have any mines?"

"I don't think so," I said. "I think it's mostly ranching, and a crossroads to feed supplies into the Tombstone Mining District."

"Hmm. No mines." Tink thought it over. "Wonder if Elfrida would be a good town?"

Chapter Eight

With the afternoon growing long across the landscape, we stopped and made camp in a gulch named Turner, about half a mile beyond a cluster of mines that, according to a broken sign lying off the side of the road, had once belonged to the Turner Mining Association. This whole place was scattered with worked-out pit mines and wooden buildings slowly turning back to dust. All of Turner Gulch pretty much looked abandoned, and we hadn't seen another soul in hours.

Waldo had not liked my going against him and volunteering to take Alice Haynes to her uncle in Elfrida. He was in one of his sulky moods again. When Waldo was upset, he never told you so straight out in words, but you always knew exactly how he was feeling by the way he got real quiet and stomped around. He banged pans, and threw down the firewood like it was infested with ants.

He was tossing wood and banging pans this evening. It was best to just ignore Waldo when he got like this, but all the same, I was anxious for him to finally settle down and light up one of his cigarettes. Whenever he did his mood usually mellowed out and things got better.

Alice was off by herself, sorting through her grief the best a little girl all alone could do. After we got the fire worked down to a nice bed of coals and the coffeepot arranged where it would stay hot, I went over and took a seat on a smooth boulder near to her.

"You holding up all right?"

She didn't look up from her folded hands where she was staring, but nodded her head.

"How old are you, Alice?"

"Eleven."

"I have a sister who is almost eleven—" I paused suddenly and shook my head. "I take that back. She *is* eleven. Anne had a birthday last month and I completely forgot about it." I was suddenly feeling down because of that, but for Alice's sake I tried to shake off the heaviness in my heart. "What happened today, well, it's a hard cross to bear, no matter what your age. At eleven you shouldn't ought to have to be burdened with it. I'm sorry."

"I don't know my uncle Ed very well."

"It will be all right. I'm sure he will take real good care of you."

"Why did those bad men kill Grandpa?"

"I don't know. This world is full of bad men. My pa would say it's because of the Fall, and Adam and Eve, and the serpent in the garden. Maybe it is. Maybe it's because some men feel they deserve a better hand than the one life has dealt them. Or maybe they just like hurting people." I grimaced as a pang of hypocrisy stabbed at me. *I was one of those bad men!* I'd just killed a man, and I'd stolen other men's goods, money, and possessions. How much lower could a man get? Without thinking about it, I touched my vest where it bulged from my stolen watch.

Alice sniffed, and dragged her sleeve across her eyes.

Right then I was so low I was almost ready to turn myself in to the law. Fortunately, Tink strolled up and went to his haunches, grinning.

"I'll bet your hair is right pretty all fixed up in long pigtails, black and shining like a raven's wing."

"I wear it that way sometimes."

I said, "If you do, you better be careful around

Tink. He's been known to dip little girls' pigtails in inkwells."

"Only done so once," Tink retorted.

"You learned your lesson that day, didn't you?" I said, recalling the incident.

"I sure did."

"What happened?" Alice asked.

"The schoolmarm, she gave me a licking with her yardstick so hard, it like to broke it in two. Then she sent me off to sit in the corner of the schoolhouse the rest of the day. Finally I had to go apologize to the girl's ma and pa and do a week of chores for the family to make 'em happy."

Tink grinned. "I never did that again. But sometimes I still give a pigtail a tug when the little girl ain't looking." He gave Alice a wink. "Don't know why. Can't hardly help myself. All you have to do is ask Howie's sister, Anne, about it. She'll tell you."

I was smiling again, and so was Alice. I didn't know what it was about Tink, but he always had the right thing to say to lift a person out of a gloomy mood.

Over at the fire Waldo said, "Come and get it—what little there is of it." We seemed to be always running shy of food.

"Hungry?" I asked.

Alice nodded.

I stood and put out a hand. She took it and allowed herself to be helped off the ground where she had been sitting. Waldo had set out four tin plates and was ladling pork and beans onto them alongside a piece of hard bread. He'd opened our last can of peaches, and we each had half a peach; luckily there were four to a can. We worked at dinner without adding much talking. We were all near starved. After a few minutes of chewing and sopping up the juice to soften the bread, Waldo said:

"Tomorrow we need to do us some grocery shopping. Anyone know what town is up ahead?"

Tink and I shook our heads.

"There aren't any towns on this road between here and Tombstone," Alice said.

"You sure?" Waldo asked.

"Pretty sure. I went once with my grandpa and a friend of his to Tombstone. We had to camp out at night 'cause there was no place to stop. Made Tombstone the next day, and we didn't come across no town in between."

Waldo frowned and reached for his box of cigarettes. "In that case, I guess that this will be our last meal until we get there."

I wasn't anxious to return to Tombstone. Tombstone was where we'd begun our life of crime. It was where we had robbed that drugstore. Where I'd got my watch. Where Waldo learned all about those cocaine cigarettes he'd been smoking ever since. But Tombstone was a big town where we could stock up on supplies, and I knew Elfrida wasn't but a day's ride east of there. I glanced at Alice. At least she'd be somewhere safe.

Alice stood, brushed the dust from her dress, and started away from us. She made for the back side of a little hill. Her shadow stretched out long in the late light, sliding across the uneven ground ahead of her as she started around it.

"Don't wander too far," Waldo said, looking relaxed now as he leaned back against his saddle. His mood had definitely improved.

"I won't," Alice called back, then took a turn around a boulder and was gone.

"Cute kid." Tink reached for the coffeepot to refill his cup.

"Yeah." I stuck out my cup, and he spilled the rest of the coffee into it. "Too bad she lost her grandpa like that. Wonder what happened to her ma and pa?"

Waldo shrugged. "That's easy enough to figure out. This is a hard land. Her pa was likely a miner. The mines can kill a man faster than a lightning strike. And women are frail creatures to begin with. Likely some sickness took her."

Douglas Hirt

"Or she died in childbirth, like my aunt Elizabeth," Tink added.

"One thing is for sure—for her age, she's seen more than her fair share of sorrows." The sky was darkening, and I was keeping an eye on the place where Alice had disappeared.

"Soon as we drop the kid off at her relations, we need to get back to work," Waldo said.

"Seems to me like we're always broke." I was amazed at how quickly we went through our money with hardly anything to show for it. "How much did you take from that old man, anyway?"

"There was four dollars and some change in the till."

"Just four dollars?" Tink said.

Waldo scowled. "Well, it ain't like I had a whole lot of time to go through the place. That old man probably had some money put away, but I couldn't look for it."

"This is worse than working the mines," Tink lamented. "At least slaving away for Carlyle, the paycheck was regular. And judging by our success so far, I do believe mining brought in more cash, too."

I gave a short laugh. "That's a mighty depressing thought, Tink. But I think you might just be right."

"Times will get better," Waldo assured us. "You just wait and see."

"Yeah, that coming from the man who once said, 'Stick with me and there will be plenty of money.'"

Waldo frowned. He obviously didn't like me throwing his own words back at him.

"Well, look at it this way. Least we don't have to bother with opening up a savings account," Tink said with a straight face.

I chuckled. Waldo grinned. Then we heard a sound like a yelp from around that little hill.

"What was that?" Waldo turned his head toward that little hill.

I don't understand why it happened, but all at once the hairs lifted clear off the back of my neck. "Alice?"

The expressions on their face said that they were thinking the same thing. I leaped to my feet, Tink and Waldo at my side, and made for that rock ahead.

"Alice?" I called before turning around it. "Alice, are you okay?"

The darkening evening remained silent, except for a soft distant rattling of gravel clattering down a slope. We plunged around the rock and looked every way for her, but the girl was gone. Ahead stood the shadowy silhouette of an old head frame, and some dilapidated miner's shacks that had long ago been abandoned. Tink started ahead, and I was right behind him.

"Alice!" he called.

"Alice?" Waldo's deeper voice boomed.

As we moved forward, I was peering hard into the shadows for any sign of movement. My view leaped across the rugged, torn-up ground, past the mounds of mine tailings, and over the slanting structures. Then I saw it right in front of us.

Tink apparently didn't see it. He'd been looking to the left, at an old winching hoist that looked sort of like a thick spider's web in the growing gloom.

"Tink!" I dove for him just as he was about to go over, catching his sleeve and hauling him to the ground. At the tips of his boots the loose gravel clattered down the steep slope and plunged over the edge. Breathlessly we waited, then heard the distant *plop, plop, plop* as the stones hit the watery bottom of a mine shaft. By the delay, I knew that shaft must have been six or seven hundred feet deep.

"Alice!" I yelled in a panic.

"Help," came a small, terrified voice from somewhere right below us.

We raced around to the other side of the dark mine shaft. Then I saw her. Alice's fingers were latched onto one of the timbers that encircled

114

the yawning drop-off; her feet swayed out in midair, dangling there.

"Hold on!" I cried, and darted back around the pit.

"You can't go down there," Waldo warned. "It's too steep."

"Don't have time to get a rope!" My brain was racing. But there was nothing we could use to get to Alice. And she could not last more than a few seconds. Already I could see her tiny fingers losing ground on the rough timber. "Take my ankles!"

"What?" Waldo sounded incredulous.

I flopped onto my belly and said it again. "Each of you grab an ankle!"

Their hands latched on to me, and I started down, sending a small avalanche of stones sliding ahead of me and plunging into the water below.

"Farther!" I said. "I can't reach her!"

"Can't go any farther!" Tink said, panic in his voice too.

I reached again, stretching my full length, but I was still two feet short of Alice. And her fingers were straining and slipping. I was normally terrified of high places, but just then that didn't seem to matter. Nothing mattered but saving Alice.

115

"I can't reach her! You have got to let me out some more!"

"We are at our ends now!" Tink came back. "Any more and we're all going to go over!"

"Then let go of me!"

"What!"

"I said let go of me. Do it! Do it now!" I felt the hesitation in their grasp. Then they did it. Gravity took over and I was suddenly sliding into that great open maw. I hit the edge and with my right hand held on for dear life. Just then Alice's grip gave out. My left arm swept out and I snatched her arm in midfall, then I held on like I've never held on to anything in my life. The jolt of her falling weight dragged me all the way over the edge, but my right hand held and then we were both hanging there, swaying over certain death, hearing a hundred pebbles raining down around us, splashing far below into that hidden water.

Alice was crying. I was straining to keep my grip and feeling near the breaking point. Above me Tink was shouting, "Howie! Howie!"

"I'm still here," I said through clenched teeth. Mustering all my strength, I lifted Alice toward the lip of the mine shaft.

"Take a hold of the edge," I told her. I couldn't hold her like that for very long. I felt Alice trying for it, then slowly her weight lessened. "Got it?"

All she could do was whimper.

"Do you have a grip?" I demanded, feeling my own hold weaken.

"Yes," came the tentative, frightened reply.

"A good grip. With both hands?"

"Yes."

"I have to let go for a moment."

"No!"

"Just for a second. Got that tight grip now?"

"Ye . . . yes."

I trusted that she did, released my hold on her, and swung around and caught the lip with my other hand. Having a two-handed hold now, and with Alice caught tightly between me and the timber shoring, I finally was able to take my first breath. My toes probed the darkness below and found a nook in one of the timbers.

"Howie—ohmygawd, Howie—you all right?" Tink was nearly incoherent.

"I'm all right . . . for the moment. Go get the rope off my saddle. I've got a good grip here."

His face disappeared in a flash, and it felt like an eternity passed before it reappeared. With the rope tied around his waist and Waldo braced above, anchoring it, Tink started down for us. He took Alice first, and with the little girl folded tightly in his arms, scrambled back up. I turned my face away from the slide of stones. Then Tink was on his way back down. His hand caught me under the arm, and I grabbed onto the rope. Between Tink's help and Waldo's pulling, they dragged me up out of that pit and I lay on the stony ground, too petrified to move at first. I ached all over, but the pain vanished when I saw Alice nearby, curled up like a frightened rag doll, her arm bent resolutely through that old, rusted, iron hoist wheel—a goodly distance from the edge of that death pit.

Every one of us was shaken to our very core. Slowly we helped each other to our feet and went back to our campfire. Waldo seemed to be in a particularly thoughtful mood afterward. He stirred the fire with a stick and mused, "Down a mine shaft like that would be great place to lose a body."

Tink and I frowned at each other.

Later, Alice came over and sat beside me. Then suddenly I was holding the little girl in my arms, feeling her sobbing quietly against my chest, releasing both pain and stress. I almost wanted to cry myself, but couldn't.

Tink tossed another stick, one that had clearly once been part of a miner's shanty, onto the fire, and I could see by the expression on his face that he was trying to come up with something clever to say. All at once he inhaled a deep, refreshing breath and stretched out his arms. "What a great night for a midnight stroll. You know, take in the stars, gaze at the moon—fall down a mine shaft."

Alice suddenly chuckled against my chest and pushed herself away. "Oh, Tink, that's a bad joke." She moved off a few feet and brushed at her dirty dress, then rubbed her tear-smudged cheeks. I could tell she was feeling better as she poured some water into a bowl to wash up in.

"She's right," Waldo said lethargically, drawing in a deep lungful of his cigarette. "A very bad joke."

"What can you expect?" I replied, giving Tink a crooked grin.

But Tink was smiling widely. I think he had gotten exactly the response he was looking for. Tink. Always the clown.

Chapter Nine

I'd been thinking the last couple days that something wasn't right, but it didn't occur to me until the next morning, after we'd been an hour or so on the road, what it was. I reined suddenly to a stop and sat there staring down at my knees.

Tink and Waldo drew up and looked back. "What's wrong, Howie?" Tink asked with the perfect innocence of a newborn baby.

My glare shifted from my knees to him, then I gave a crooked smile. "That's pretty childish of you, Mr. Dobie Tinkerman," I said, sounding an awful lot like my mother.

"What?"

"Don't *what* me. When did you do it?"

"Do what?" He was playing the part real good,

pretending he didn't know what I was talking about.

"What are you driving at, Howie?" Waldo asked sternly, not in any mood for delays or horseplay.

"I've been short-stirruped. And there is only one character here I know of who would pull such a prank."

Tink gave me a blank look.

"You did it, didn't you?"

"I never done such a thing ... Well," he grinned, "at least not to you. And not for a long time."

"Don't give me that." I reached back for Alice's hand and lowered her to the ground. She held on to me like flypaper. Since last night's incident, she'd become real clingy. I reckon I couldn't blame her. I still broke out in a sweat whenever I thought about how close we'd both come to St. Peter's Pearly Gates. And I guess what had me worried most is what old St. Pete would have said if I had showed up there last night. I didn't want to ponder the possibilities, considering the sort of life I'd been living lately.

I swung down off my horse and gave Tink a withering stare.

"I didn't do it. Honest!" Tink protested, dismounting too.

"You're the only one here who would," I said, working the buckle and letting the strap down two notches. "How long have I been riding around like this, with my knees up in the air and not knowing it? When did you do it, Tink?" I stopped all at once and stared at the leather. The fold to where I had lowered the stirrups to the leather was stiff and unyielding.

"See, I never moved your stupid stirrups," Tink shot back.

I was momentarily dumbfounded. "But if you didn't . . ."

"Looks to me like you've been sprouting, Howie," Waldo said, leaning forward in his saddle, forearm resting upon the pommel.

I stared at Tink, suddenly realizing I wasn't looking up at him anymore. If anything, he had shrunk an inch. "But . . . but when did it happen?"

"It's been happening right along," Waldo said. "Only, you haven't noticed. Not until you'd grown enough to see the change."

"Turn around. Take your hat off." We stood back to back, and I measured us. Sure enough, my hand skimmed over his hair by at least an inch.

Tink laughed at the astonished look on my face. "I think you owe someone an apology."

Heat rose into my cheeks. "I reckon I do. Sorry, Tink."

He laughed again and went back to his horse. I finished lowering the stirrup straps, amazed at the change I hadn't even noticed, and remounted with Alice once again behind me.

All that morning I thought about it. Curiously, I was thinking of Pa too, and wondering if I was as tall as he. It was funny, but try as I might, I couldn't recall his face clearly. I could see Ma as if she had been captured in one of Mr. Eastman's Kodak boxes, but Pa's face seemed to fade behind a cloud. And I was having trouble with Anne and Beth too. I still hadn't written to them. I realized suddenly that the day after tomorrow was going to be my birthday, and I'd been away from them for a year. Pondering on the swiftness of time, I realized something else too. We were just leaving the old century behind. The calendar had turned over to 1900 last January first, and we were in a new century! I hadn't thought a whole lot about it until just then.

Tombstone hadn't changed much in the year we'd been away. Maybe there were a few more poles along Allen Street strung up with an ever-growing mare's nest of telephone wires. Bell's invention seemed to be spreading across the

West like wildfire. But that was about the only change.

We were all hungrier than marooned sailors, and at the first place we came to, we turned our horses into the hitching rail and headed inside. It was a small, clean café, narrow as a toothpick with a single row of tables down the wall. One row was about all that could be squeezed in there. A man in a greasy apron came from a back room and told us that the menu today was boiled beef and potatoes fried up with onions. We took it, grateful for anything to fill up the empty places in our bellies.

Afterward, Waldo, Tink, and I lingered at the table drinking coffee. Alice settled for water and seemed happy with it.

Waldo said, "We've almost gotten you to your uncle Ed, Alice. Tomorrow we'll be in Elfrida."

"Do I have to go?" she asked.

Tink grinned. "Don't tell me you're growing comfortable with the likes of us three desert rats?"

Alice smiled faintly but didn't reply.

"You belong with your aunt and uncle," I said.

"I know, Howie." She replied as if resigned to the inevitable.

"Besides, we move around a lot," Waldo

added. "And life with us can be on the dangerous side."

I caught his hidden meaning in that, even
though Alice only saw the obvious.

"But Howie would always be there to help
me. And you seem to know the answer to everything, Waldo."

Waldo gave one of his rare, tight grins. "I appreciate the vote of confidence, Alice. But like
Howie says, you belong with your aunt and uncle."

Alice let it drop. She was only eleven, but she
was grown up enough to see the truth in that.

We left the café and lingered on the boardwalk a moment, shading our eyes from the
morning glare.

"Wonder what time it is," Waldo said.

Tink shrugged. "I don't know, but the sun is
over the yardarm." He grinned. "You know
what that means?"

"It means the bar is open, boys, and I've got
cash in my pocket." Waldo jingled the coins.

"Well, while you two go exploring the local
saloons, better pass me some of that money
what's burning a hole in your pocket, Waldo. I
need to buy a few things, and I don't think a
saloon is anyplace for Alice to be hanging out."

Waldo fished a dollar out of his pocket and
handed it over. "There isn't much. Don't spend

it all in one place, Howie." He laughed, and the two of them headed for the nearest watering hole.

Alice and I found a general mercantile, and I bought a pad of writing paper, a pencil, and an envelope. Then we discovered a drugstore with a soda fountain, and each of us had a Coca-Cola. Alice had never tasted one before, and she giggled as the fizz tickled her nose. I found that I liked being with Alice. She reminded me of Anne and Beth, but mostly of Anne.

"What are you doing?" she asked me when I opened the tablet and began a letter.

"Writing a letter to my family," I said. "I haven't written in an awful long time."

"Why don't you go visit them, Howie? Bisbee is not so far from here."

I couldn't tell her why. How could I admit that for the last year I'd been living the life of a common criminal? How could I go home and lie straight out to my ma and pa and the girls? I couldn't. And even if I tried, Pa would see through it almost at once.

"I will, one of these days, but we travel so much it's hard to get back. In the meantime, I'll write them a letter, just to let them know I'm all right." In truth, I'd been thinking mightily about my mortality since last night, and for some reason I just felt compelled to write a letter to my family today.

Alice accepted my excuse without question and went back to sipping her Coca-Cola through the paper soda straw. I penciled a few lines, telling how we were doing fine, seeing the country and all. I didn't say the only country we'd seen so far had been hot and dry Arizona Territory mining country—the very land I had so desperately wanted to escape. I told them that Tink was well, and that Waldo was clever and always able to find us work. I left it at that—neither a lie nor the truth, but something in between, though deep down in my heart those words pricked at a sleeping conscience.

Afterward, we walked to the post office, where I posted the letter to Bisbee, then we strolled on down to look at the big courthouse, which had been built only a few years earlier. The OK Corral was nearby, so we went there next and peered over the adobe walls. A couple horses were working on a pile of hay. There was no evidence of the famous gunfight that had taken place between the Earps, Doc Holliday, and the Clanton gang.

I was struck by the thought of all those men dying, of all that blood spilled, and yet today life in the corral was going on as normal, as if none of it had ever happened. I thought of last night again, and how very little would have changed if Alice and I had ended up in the bottom of that mine shaft. Life goes on, and one person really doesn't make much of a difference. Oh, some do, but not many. George Washington, Thomas Jefferson, Martin Luther, and a few others have left their marks. But for the rest of us . . .

I was being more introspective than usual as we headed back into town. I might have stayed that way all day except that all of a sudden Alice and I found ourselves among a bunch of people crowding along the boardwalk, watching something happening out in the street.

"Wonder what's going on?" I said, rising to my toes for a peek over the heads in front of us.

"What is it?" she asked.

"Can't see." I took her hand, and we shouldered our way through the crowd.

"It's Waldo!" Alice cried.

Sure enough, it was Waldo pacing out into the middle of the street. At first I wondered what he was up to. Then I spied the other fellow, a little farther off, making his way out there too. My heart took a leap and landed plum in the center of my throat.

"Waldo's gotten himself in some kind of trouble this time," I said, my view darting between the two men. I strained to hear above the murmuring throng.

I spied Tink on the boardwalk across the street, clutching a porch upright as if he needed it for support. I couldn't make him out clearly through the crowd, but there was no hiding that stretched-eye stare of disbelief and fear.

"What's happening?" Alice asked.

"Looks like Waldo and that fellow are about to settle some difference between 'em with six-shooters."

"A shoot-out?"

"Hush. I'm trying to hear." And so were the rest of the gawkers, for as soon as the stranger spoke you could hear a feather drop.

"You can back out of this anytime you want, kid."

"It was you who started it. You back out." Waldo's voice was easy, and there was a cool confidence that makes a man's blood run cold.

"Why don't both you boys break it up?" a voice from the crowd rang out.

Someone else said, "Think about what you two are doing. This is nineteen hundred, for pity sakes. We're trying for statehood. Think about what the people back in Washington will say when they hear there are still shootings in the middle of the street, like it was still twenty years ago when the Earps and Clantons were running this place!"

But neither Waldo nor the other fellow paid any heed to that.

"I'm giving you one last chance to back down with only an apology, kid."

Waldo swept back the tails of his frock coat, unruffled, and casually extracted a cigar from an inside pocket. He wetted it between his lips, then grinned around the cigar and reached inside another pocket for a match.

"Well?" the fellow demanded. "What will it be?"

"Take your best shot, peckerwood."

"You sonuvabitch." The man's hand inched for the gun, but since Waldo was in the middle of lighting up a smoke, the fellow took a more deliberate approach and rested his hand upon the grip of the Colt, waiting.

I caught my breath. I'd seen this played out once before . . . I'd been that fellow down the street! All at once the spring let loose. Waldo dropped the match as his hand leaped for the gun. It cleared leather in a heartbeat, and the boom jarred my teeth. The fellow lurched backward and landed in a twisted heap. He didn't even move a twitch. Waldo's bullet had snuffed out his life before he had hit the ground.

For a moment all I heard was the whisper of a hot wind that swirled the gun smoke about Waldo and dispersed it against the sea of faces across the street. Slowly a murmur stirred, then swelled, and a couple of men cautiously approached the body.

"He's dead!"

No one got too close to Waldo as he stood there, revolver still in his hand. His face was stone, and his dark eyes glistening chunks of polished obsidian. Alice's grip upon my hand had become very tight, and her eyes had grown bigger than coat buttons.

Then, as if coming out of some terrible trance, Waldo took in a sudden breath and casually slipped his gun back into the leather.

I was about to go to him when from the crowd two men stepped into view, carrying sawed-off shotguns. They moved right out to Waldo, those guns pointed at him, and sunlight glinting off the polished nickel badges pinned to their shirts. Quick as a saddle-shy bronc, they braced Waldo, took his gun, and said, "Better come with us, boy."

"It was a fair fight, Sheriff," someone spoke up. But the lawmen paid no heed as they hauled Waldo off to the jailhouse.

"Why are they taking him away?" I asked a man standing nearby.

"Tombstone's got ordinances about carrying guns. That young buck will likely face a judge for murder, and probably a half-dozen other

131

charges." He gave a chuckle. "There's a gallows built out behind the courthouse, and it's in sore need of some practical use, or the taxpayers will have something to say the next time the city wants to spend more of their hard-earned money."

I was stunned by his words. "But it was a fair fight."

Waldo facing a judge! A hanging!

I'd never heard of a man being arrested for fighting a fair fight. But then, I kept forgetting that the old ways were passing us by . . . and Waldo and Tink and me, we were men living out of our time.

The man I was speaking to only shrugged his shoulders. Now that the show was over, the crowd was breaking up, and he headed back into one of the doorways from where he had come.

Across the street, Tink was gawking with confusion and concern plastered across his face—probably looking pretty much as I appeared to him at the moment. With Alice in tow, I started toward him, feeling suddenly like we were all in a small boat cut adrift of the shore.

Chapter Ten

"I'd never seen Waldo use his gun before—not for real, at least," Tink said as the three of us sat around a table in the drugstore, drinking root beers.

"He sure is fast, but look where it got him. Jail! And facing a judge, and maybe even a hangman." I took another pull at the soda straw, too upset to taste what I was drinking.

"It wasn't his fault. It was that other man's fault! He reached for his gun first. I saw it." Alice's wide brown eyes flashed with indignation. It surprised me that she'd taken so strongly to defending him.

"I saw it too, and maybe it wasn't his fault," I said, "but that other fellow is dead. Can't stand a dead man before a judge."

Her mouth tightened and her eyes flashed.

"Maybe so, Howie, but Alice is right. It wasn't Waldo's fault. Shoot, I was there when that fellow began badgering us. He was half drunk and figured just because he was bigger and older than us he could boot us out of our table and take it for his own. Waldo tried to talk to him, but he wouldn't listen."

"Doesn't seem like much of a reason to get in a gunfight over," I replied. "Shoot, if he wanted that table that bad, I'd have given it up."

"Maybe you would have, and I would have too, Howie. But you know how Waldo gets when he thinks someone is trying to best him."

"Yeah. And he's been upset lately because his Fri—" I stopped just in time, nearly forgetting that Alice was sitting there. "I mean, because he hasn't been able to reach certain goals he's set for himself."

Tink knew what I was referring to. He'd caught my hasty recovery and surreptitious glance at Alice, and let that particular subject die. She didn't seem to pick up on it, which was a relief.

"So, what do we do now?"

I shook my head. "Wish I knew."

"I think we should go to the sheriff and tell him to let Waldo go," Alice said.

"I don't think that will do a lot of good," I said.

"Maybe my uncle Ed can help?"

"I doubt it," Tink said.

Alice frowned.

"Maybe we oughta take Alice to her uncle, then come back and wait for the trial," I suggested after a few moments of silence.

Tink's straw growled as he sucked up the last few drops of root beer. "That's sorta like doing nothing at all."

"What's there to do?"

"We got to start thinking for ourselves now, Howie. What would Waldo do if it was you in there instead?"

I gave a short laugh. "Probably ride off without a second thought."

"Would not."

"Uh-uh," Alice added emphatically, shaking her head.

There hadn't been a moment of hesitation between the two of them.

"I'll tell you what he'd do," Tink said. "He'd make plans. Waldo is always making plans."

"What kind of plans?"

Tink leaned closer and lowered his voice. "He'd be making plans to bust you out of that jail."

Alice was leaning forward too, her brown eyes wide with curiosity. She looked from Tink to me. "Can we do that?"

"We?" I asked.

"I'm going to help too."

"We'll see about that." I considered Tink's notion and knew it was what we had to do. If nothing else, a daring jailbreak might finally put the Fritz Gang's name in the newspapers. That would be pure frosting atop Waldo's cake! I was shocked at how fast I warmed to the idea, but it was perfect, and I suddenly had the whole thing before me as if someone had sketched a picture inside my head, showing me how it was all going to come about.

"I got it!" I gave a careful look around the store to make sure no one was near then we put our heads together. "Tonight, after the sheriff has gone home, we'll go in through the back door, free Waldo, and quietly leave town."

"But won't the back door be locked?" Alice asked, sensibly.

I gave Tink a knowing smirk. "Maybe it will, but Tink and me, we've sometimes been able to unlock a locked door." It was one of the benefits of our trade. The number of doors left unlatched had never been enough to support us, so over the months we'd learned to pick a lock or two. It wasn't all that hard once you got the hang of it.

I considered Alice. "If we do this, you'll have to promise never to tell anyone. Is that clear?"

Alice crossed her heart. "I won't tell anyone, Howie. Promise. But maybe my uncl—"

"Not even your uncle!"

"All right. If you think so," she allowed half-heartedly.

"I think so. Now, we'll have to bring the horses with us so we can make a fast getaway if anyone see us. Right?"

"Right," Tink rejoined.

I nodded. "I think we oughta go scout out that back door right now."

We found the sheriff's office and strolled innocently past it, then ducked down an alleyway and turned left. It was a brick-and-frame building with a sturdy back door that at the moment was held open by a short stick, allowing a breeze to circulate through. I kept an eye peeled while Tink examined the lock. It wasn't anything fancy.

Once we started moving again, he said, "I can open that easy as prying the lid off a can of sardines!"

That sort of confidence always made me squirm a little, but I just gave Tink a grin and a nod. "Then tonight we'll bust Waldo out of that sardine can."

Tink appreciated my small stab at humor.

* * *

That night we huddled near a campfire not far outside of Tombstone, waiting for time to pass. We wanted to be good and sure no one was awake when we broke Waldo out of that jailhouse, so we bided our time. As the hours went by, we listened to the far-off chatter of coyotes and the soft, questioning voice of a nearby owl. Around ten o'clock, Alice curled up in a blanket and almost instantly fell asleep.

"Poor kid. She's all worn out," I said softly, sipping the last of our coffee, listening to the fire crackle.

"I sort of admire her spunk."

"The kid's got grit."

Tink made a face. "Yeah, and so does this coffee." He tossed out the remains and peered inside his cup.

I'd been thinking about all that had happened the last couple days and feeling unsettled. Maybe it was having killed a man. I hadn't intended to kill anyone, and he was sort of shooting at me, which made it self-defense. But just the same, the experience was weighing heavy.

"You happy with the way we've been going, Tink?" I asked all at once, hearing an unexpected serious tone to my voice.

"What do you mean?"

"I mean with what we are doing." With a glance at Alice, I lowered my voice. "You know, robbing folks? And then what happened the other day, and this afternoon with Waldo and all?"

"Sure, it's a great life."

I frowned.

"Well, sometimes," Tink added more soberly. "Why? You having second thoughts now?"

"Have been for a long while. I don't know, Tink. It just don't wear comfortable like I thought it would. I don't know why. Can't explain it any better than that."

"You thinking of pulling out?"

"The notion has crossed my mind. But what would I do? I've got no money. And I can't go back home, not having lived the kind of life we done for the last year. If Ma and Pa ever found out, it would be a horrible blow to them. And the girls, I don't think I could ever look them in the face and not feel mighty guilty."

Tink grimaced, and his bold facade came down. "Sometimes I feel the same way. Wouldn't want to admit it in front of Waldo, though. He thinks this here is a great life, except that no one takes his Fritz Gang seriously. That stings him hard."

"Wonder why it matters so to him?"

Tink rolled his shoulders and poked at the coals with a stick.

"Know what I'm thinking?"

"What?" He didn't look up from the fire.

"I'm thinking that if I ever get any money ahead—you know, enough cash to live on for a few months until I can find some decent work—then I'm going to quit this life and maybe look for that good town you keep talking about."

His head came up, and there was a grin on his face. "Yeah, that would be the ticket. I'd like that."

"But what would Waldo do?" I wondered.

"Waldo would just keep on being Waldo, I guess. He'd pick up other partners."

"Wouldn't want to hurt his feelings or anything."

"You got to do what's right for you, Howie."

"Would you come along with me?"

"Sure I would. We're partners." He grinned. "Besides, who's gonna keep you out of trouble if I'm not around?"

I laughed quietly in the dark. "Yeah? And just who was it who saved you from tumbling down that mine shaft?"

Tink smirked. "I saw that mine shaft. I was just testing you."

We woke Alice sometime after midnight and rode back to Tombstone. The town was mostly asleep, except for a couple saloons whose lights spilled out across Allen Street. Piano music wafted on a cooling breeze that made the evening right pleasant. Most of the buildings were dark, and only a few houses a couple blocks off the main street showed any kind of light. To our relief, the sheriff's office appeared closed up for the night, its lawmen hopefully at home and sawing logs in their beds. The alley was dark and deserted, and we dismounted, stepping quietly over to the back door.

"Keep an eye out for trouble," I whispered to Alice, putting our horses in her charge. She led them to the tight passage that ran between the buildings and opened onto Allen Street, and stopped at the corner, dividing her attention between us and the street.

Tink extracted a sliver of metal that had worked in the past for picking locks and began softly probing the interior of the lock, his face contorted with concentration, his ear pressed near the opening.

"There might be someone sleeping inside," I warned.

"I'm being quiet as I can."

I glanced up and down the alley nervously.

Tink fumbled around for about five minutes with no luck.

"Easy as prying a lid off a sardine can?"

He ignored me.

"Let me try," I said finally, certain that any

141

moment someone was going to appear and run us off—like what happened the last time we were in Tombstone, when we broke into that drugstore. I worked at the lock a few minutes with no better luck.

"This ain't no regular candy-store lock, Tink."

"What are we going to do?"

I stood and gave the heavy iron handle a pull. There was about a quarter-inch play in the door, and that was all.

"Maybe we can pry it?" he suggested.

"With what?"

Tink shrugged.

I considered the problem, my view wandering over to where Alice was waiting with our horses. That's when an idea hit me, and I waved Alice over to us.

"What?" Tink demanded.

"We'll put a rope through that handle and pull the door off."

"Pull it off?" Tink looked dubious, but it was the only play left in a game where we'd run out of cards. "All right, let's give it a try."

I ran an end of my rope through the heavy iron handle and over to two of the horses, wrapping it around their pommels. Then I took it back again once more through the handle, where I tied it off in a big square knot.

"All right, now!" I whispered.

Tink took charge of the animals, urging them forward. I gripped the rope and lent a hand. Tink kept up the pressure, clucking softly as he pulled on the reins. I had planted a foot against the wall and was straining at the ropes, about to bust all the veins in my neck, when something cracked. The wood jamb splintered and the door burst open with a horrible sound.

We looked all around, terrified someone might have heard. We hadn't a minute to waste. "Untie the horses," I said, and slipped inside, my revolver tight in my sweating hand.

"What's happening?" a voice called sleepily from the darkness.

I froze.

"Who's there?" another asked through a yawn. A couple men in a jail cell just ahead were coming groggily awake.

"Waldo?" I called, moving in among the cell blocks.

"Howie? Over here." Waldo leaped off a cot and came to the bars. "I knew you and Tink wouldn't leave me here."

"Where are the keys?"

"In there somewhere." He stabbed a finger at the connecting door. I hurried into the office, fumbled around in the dark, and finally spied a ring of keys hanging off a nail on the wall. Back in the cell block I tried half a dozen before one

143

finally clicked over and Waldo's door swung open.

"Wait here." In a flash he darted into the main office.

"Hey, kid, how about opening our door too," one of the other prisoners said.

"I . . . I don't think so," I said uncertainly.

"What can it hurt?" he countered.

I heard Waldo rustling through some drawers in the other room.

"Come on," another implored, "spring us, kid. I'm facing the rope if you don't!"

I saw his face in a slash of moonlight from a window high up in the wall. It was round and full, and his skull was cue-ball smooth. I noticed that one eye seemed lower than the other, and then I saw the scar that cut across his left eyebrow and down his cheek. His full mouth took a sudden downward tilt that shaped the face into a grotesque mask in the shadowy moonlight.

"If you don't let us go too, we'll tell the sheriff who sprung Waldo. I've a sharp eye for details. I'll give him your description. Your face will be on Wanted posters from here to Denver City!"

Waldo reappeared, buckling his six-shooter around his narrow hips. "Let's fly!" he said, heading for the back door.

I hesitated. The very last thing I wanted was

for my picture to appear on a Wanted poster. What if Ma and Pa saw it?

"Howie, let's get going," Tink's urgent voice called from outside.

"Howie, is it?" That scar arched upward and those thick lips formed a wicked smile. "Now I have a name to give the sheriff along with the description."

That was all I needed to hear. I tossed the ring of keys through the bars to him and rushed out of that building like it was on fire.

Chapter Eleven

We found Waldo's horse down at the livery and slipped out of Tombstone in the dead of night. I was fretting over those other men I let out, but after thinking it over some, decided it would work to our advantage. In the morning when the break-out was discovered, the sheriff would have to puzzle over whose friends did the deed. He might just conclude it was those other men's buddies that busted into his office. That would send him sniffing a trail away from us.

Daylight found us on the road to Elfrida with Tombstone many dusty miles behind us. I was still checking the empty double tracks over my shoulder almost as often as I was looking ahead, but no one was following us. As the morning drew on, I became more confident.

Tink and Alice hadn't said much. Waldo had done most of the talking, bragging about how no jail cell could ever hold him.

I had the impression that the one we'd just busted him out of had been doing a dandy job of holding him, and that Waldo really had taken no material part in the breakout at all. But if he wanted to feel it was his prowess that had freed him, so be it. I wasn't in the mood to correct him.

We came to Elfrida a little before noon. It wasn't much of a town: one main street with two or three others running parallel to it, and two or three more cutting crosswise. There was the usual collection of business storefronts, and a couple saloons tossed in for good measure.

East of town was a big tent of the sort a traveling preacher might have set up. Today being Saturday, I figured tonight and tomorrow morning it would be filled to the gills with miners and ranchers and businessmen hungry for the sort of food rarely served up in this town's cafés and hotel restaurants. If Pa were here he'd likely be first in line, I mused—if it wasn't his turn to stand in the doorway of our church and shake hands.

"This looks like a good town," Tink noted optimistically as we rode in from the west.

"Good for outlaws and drunks and gunmen

147

of the meanest reputation, from what I hear," Waldo replied offhandedly.

"We better not hang around here very long," I said. "Word of your escape won't take long to get out." Alice's grip briefly tightened around my waist, then relaxed. "Remember you promised not to tell anyone about last night. We can get into big trouble if you do."

"I already crossed my heart, Howie," she reminded me.

"That's right, you did."

"Where does your uncle Ed live?" Waldo asked.

"I don't know. I've never been to his house," she said.

"He should be easy to find in a town this size."

It wasn't much of a town, and it wasn't very busy. A huge warehouse stood off a ways, and it appeared to have the most activity this time of day. I angled across the road toward it and hailed a man just coming out of the big sliding door, carrying a stuffed burlap sack on his shoulder. He was a solidly built fellow who looked more than capable of lifting and moving heavy freight or swinging a hammer against an anvil.

"Looking for a man named Ed Berger. You couldn't tell me where I might find him?"

He leaned forward and pitched the sack over

the side of a dray. It landed with a heavy thump among some others already loaded. Straightening and slinging the sweat from his brow, he asked, "Deputy Marshal Berger? You might start looking at the sheriff's office." He pointed up the road. "It's up that way, just around the corner.

Marshal? My heartbeat quickened, though I stayed cool on the outside. "Thanks." We turned our horses and started up the street.

"Your uncle is a marshal?"

"Yes," came the reply from behind me.

Tink and Waldo were staring at me from beneath gathering brows.

"Wonderful idea, Howie, volunteering to bring her," Waldo said tightly.

"What sort of marshal is he?" Tink asked, a tentative note in his voice.

"A United States deputy marshal, I think," Alice replied.

"A federal marshal?" Tink croaked.

"Wonderful," Waldo said again.

I tried to look on the bright side. After all, in spite of Waldo's best efforts, we'd never made much of a reputation for ourselves. Marshal Ed Berger probably had never even heard of the Fritz Gang. And that we had rescued his niece and were seeing her safely to family would certainly go a long way to dousing any suspicion he might have . . . I hoped.

The sheriff's office was located about a block off the main street, down one of the side avenues. It sat on a big corner lot with no other buildings nearby. We screwed up our courage and went inside. A man with a tin star on his chest was snoozing in a chair, his boot heels propped on a scarred desk. He came awake with a start when we stepped through the doorway, tipping his hat back from his eyes and blinking sleepily at us.

"What can I do for you boys?"

"We're looking for Marshal Ed Berger, Sheriff," I said.

"Ain't here. Can't you see?" His thumb jabbed at the second desk, which was presently unoccupied.

"When will he be back?"

"Whenever he gets the notion, I suspect. Can I help you?"

"No, we really need to see the marshal," Waldo said.

"Then you might want to try his house. To the left two blocks, then take a right. It's an adobe. The only one like it. Can't miss it."

We didn't miss it. Berger's house was the only one made of mud. The other four homes on the street were frame, painted white, with little covered porches out front. There were half a dozen newly planted trees along the street, and several of the homes had vegetable patches out back behind low picket fences. I watched a couple goats busily shoving their noses between the pickets, and a lone cow pulling at a clump of dried grass.

Berger's squat adobe was painted pink and had a long covered porch out front with an *olla* and an iron dipper hanging from the beams. An old cottonwood tree shaded the west side of the weedy lot, leaving the house temporarily stranded in full sunlight this time of day.

We dismounted. A rooster crowed at us from the coping around the flat roof, while five or six hens scurried around the corner. Tink and Waldo led the horses into the shade of the tree. I took Alice's hand, and we climbed the single step to the porch and knocked on the door.

"Nervous?" I asked, standing there and waiting.

"A little."

I was nervous a lot, but I didn't tell her that. I reminded myself that there were many advantages to *not* having a reputation.

"Hello?" A woman had opened the door. She stood about five feet two inches, was middle-aged with brunette hair faintly streaked with gray. Her green eyes moved from me to Alice and then back to me. Then all of a sudden she shot Alice a second look.

"Alice!"

"Aunt Gladys."

"What a surprise. What are you doing here? Where is your grandpa?" Gladys Berger must have read the answer to that in both our faces. "Something has happened to him?"

Alice's mouth began to quiver. I said, "I'm afraid that Mr. Haynes is dead."

"Dead?" Gladys's hand leaped to her throat and a small, startled gasp escaped her lips.

"What is it, dear?" came a husky voice from inside.

She turned back. "It's Father. He's . . ." her voice faltered, "he's dead."

Alice, Gladys, and Ed sat close together on a faded tapestry settee while Waldo, Tink, and I faced them in three hard, straight-back chairs. Gladys and Alice had had themselves a good cry while Ed, a tall, bulky man with a sunburned face, graying hair, and a gentle way about him, had consoled them as best he could. I felt sorry for Ed, because it looked an awful lot like he wanted to cry too. But of course, he couldn't allow that to happen—not in front of the three of us men. And he had to be strong for both the females' sakes, too.

Afterward, Marshal Ed Berger took us out behind the house and asked for the details as best we could remember them. Between the three of us we fleshed out the incident, leaving out the true reason why we had been there.

"Do you remember their faces?" he asked. "Could you pick 'em out of a stack of Wanted posters?"

We looked at each other and shook our heads.

"It happened so fast," I said. "I didn't have a good look. But that one who was killed, maybe Sheriff Hackler can identify him for you?"

"Pat Hackler, you say his name is?"

"That's right," Tink replied.

Berger pursed his lips and thought about that. Then he shook his head. "I don't know the man, but I'll send off a wire tonight to Tombstone to see if anyone there knows where he can be found."

"I wouldn't wire the sheriff in Tombstone," Waldo said quickly, a flash of concern in his eyes. "We were a long piece off from there. You'd have better luck trying Tubac. Your father-in-law's store was not far from Tubac."

"That's right," Berger said thoughtfully. "Maybe this Hackler fellow is a lawman there in Tubac." He paused, and a puzzled look darkened his face. "Wonder if they have a wire stretched to Tubac?"

153

"Most likely," Tink said quickly, apparently nervous, like Waldo, about what news a telegram to Tombstone might bring in return. "Folks are stringing up wires faster than the wire factories can turn 'em out. That's why copper mining is booming in this part of the Territory. One of these days you won't be able to look up into the sky without having to do so past a jumble of copper threads. Like looking through one of my old socks that Ma had filled full of darns."

Berger grinned at Tink's imagery. "Ain't that the truth of it, son?"

Gladys Berger came from the back door, wiping her hands on her apron. Her eyes were puffy and red, but she had shut off the tears for the moment. "I was wondering if you three gentlemen would like to stay for dinner? It's the least we can offer you, for going so far out of your way to bring Alice safely to us." She glanced up at her husband, who immediately nodded his approval.

I hadn't had a real home-cooked meal in over a year. I jumped at the opportunity, and Tink and Waldo weren't far behind me in saying we'd be pleased to stay for evening victuals.

"Good." Gladys managed a brief smile and went back inside the house.

"She's a strong woman," I said.

"That she is." Berger drew in a long breath and let it slowly out. "Dinner will be a while. In the meantime, I'll go send off that telegram. You wouldn't mind looking through some Wanted posters for me, on the outside chance there might be a face among them you'd recognize?"

We walked back to the sheriff's office, where we startled the sleepy sheriff awake again.

"Afternoon, Marshal," he said, swinging his feet off the desk.

"Afternoon, Matt. Mind if I have a look at those Wanted posters?"

"Go ahead. You know where they are." Matt watched the big man go to a cabinet and retrieve a stack of posters. "Something the matter, Ed?"

"Just got word that Gladys's father has been murdered."

The news stunned Matt. He shook his head. "Sorry to here that. How is Gladys taking it?"

"As you'd expect."

"Do you know who done it?"

"No. Not yet."

"Anything me and Doris can do for her?"

"Nothing right now. These three gentlemen were there when it happened. They brought our niece to us. Er, this here is Howie and Tink and Waldo. Matt Tingley, our sheriff. Matt's been kind enough to let me use a corner of his office."

We pumped hands with the sheriff.

"I was hoping they might find a face among all these." Berger dropped the stack onto the unoccupied desk. "I'm going to leave them here while I go and send a telegram."

"Sure, Ed. You boys just make yourselves at home."

"I'll be back." Berger strode out the door, Matt told us to take our time, so we gathered around the sheaf of Wanted posters and began paging through them one by one. I was half afraid that somehow my picture would turn up among them, but that was boastful thinking at best. There wasn't a mention of the Fritz Gang, and not a single likeness of any one of us. I was mightily relieved, although I knew a picture of Waldo would have brightened his day considerably. But it wasn't to be—at least not yet.

The office was about the size of our little house back in Bisbee. There were two flat-iron cells at the back where our bedrooms would have been. The office occupied the front part— where our kitchen and parlor would have stood. A couple of windows spilled light onto the desk where we were flipping through posters. There was a cot in one corner, for overnight guard duty, I reckoned, and a rack on the wall with three Winchester rifles and a pair of shotguns—

one with a sawed-off barrel. A bulletin board on the wall across from Matt's desk held some flyers and notes, and an announcement for "Brother Harold's Revival Meeting" set for that night and the next, and Monday evening too—for those reluctant souls, I mused. If Pa were here, he'd probably have attended all three services!

It had been a long time since I'd cast a shadow across the doorway of a church, canvas or otherwise. I had a sudden, odd urge to go see what Brother Harold was all about, but I put it down right quick. The inside of a church was no place for a sinner like me.

"I hear Elfrida can be a pretty rough place," Waldo said to Matt as the sheriff shuffled papers about his desktop.

"We sometimes get desperadoes on the move. We're sitting right on the crossroads from Willcox to Douglas and Tombstone. A man on the run trying to make Mexico, or banditos from down south coming north, they usually all stop here in Elfrida."

"Any big names?"

"A few. But mostly they're small-time crooks and thieves, and a few murderers. The really big desperadoes avoid us because we have a full-time sheriff, me, and a U.S. deputy marshal, Ed, posted here."

"Why so much law for such a small place?"

"Location."

"You mean, being a crossroads?"

He nodded. "Not only do we get a lot of folks passing through, but this is the route the pay wagons take for the Tombstone and Douglas mines. Protecting them, that's Ed's job, since they're hauling federal property, mainly minted gold." He grinned. "A man can't hardly ever get enough of those shiny eagles, though a lot try."

Waldo laughed. "Ain't that the truth."

Amen, I thought.

Marshal Ed Berger returned after about an hour, saying that a reply to his telegram should be coming later that day. He was disappointed that we hadn't pulled a face out of that stack for him, but said that he hadn't really expected us to anyway.

He took us around to the main street and bought us each a beer at the Crystal Slipper Saloon. Then he thanked us again for helping Alice and bringing word of Franklin Haynes's death. I liked Ed Berger right from the start and felt that Alice would be raised right by both him and Gladys. I don't know why I was so concerned about the little girl, except that she reminded me of Anne. I was feeling cut off from my family, missing them more than I had in months. Maybe that was why.

When we left the Crystal Slipper I stood a moment, peering at the big tent on the edge of town.

"Meeting tonight. Want to go?" Berger offered, seeing me staring at it.

"No . . . no, thanks. I think I'll pass," I said.

He only grinned and nodded, and we all went back to his house.

Chapter Twelve

Dinner was wonderful, although the mood was gloomy, with Gladys on the verge of tears the whole time. Alice was a big help to her, and I reckoned the two of them were hitting it off. Ed Berger seemed somber and distracted. I suspected he was wondering how to run down the killers who had done this to them. After the dishes had been cleared, Berger inquired into what the three of us did for a living.

Waldo was quick as ever. While I was still stammering for an answer, he said, "We're businessmen, looking around for a good town to set up shop."

"Businessmen? Hmm, what sort of business?"

"We haven't made a final decision on that,"

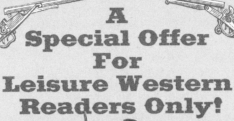

Get Four Books Totally
FREE* –
A Value between
$16 and $20

PLEASE RUSH
MY FOUR FREE*
BOOKS TO ME
RIGHT AWAY!

LeisureWestern Book Club
P.O. Box 6613
Edison, NJ 08818-6613

AFFIX
STAMP
HERE

he continued glibly. "Tink and Howie, they're leaning toward a general mercantile store. Me, on the other hand, I'd fancy owning a saloon, something like the Crystal Slipper."

"Walt Henderson does a good business with the Crystal Slipper," Berger said. "But then, Peter Whorley's mercantile shop is a good solid income producer too, isn't that right, Gladys?" he called toward the kitchen.

"I don't know. Helen never talks much about Peter's business."

There was a sob in her voice, and he grimaced. I figured out that Berger had asked her that only to try to put her mind on something other than her grief.

Just then there was a knock on the door. Berger let in a woman carrying a cake. She instantly took his hand and said how sorry she was to hear of the death of Gladys's father, then she bustled over and gave Gladys a big hug.

"That is Doris Tingley. Matt Tingley's wife," he told us, closing the door to the evening shadows. He went around the parlor, lighting lamps and drawing the shades, then brought out cups and a coffeepot. Gladys carried in the cake. The arrival of Doris Tingley brought on a fresh bout of tears that lasted all of twenty minutes while we ate our cake and sipped our coffee.

Waldo was getting antsy. I figured it was being cooped up all day with a lawman that was doing it. All at once he stood and said, "I think I'll just step outside and smoke me a cigarette."

I knew he'd be more relaxed when he came back.

Doris volunteered to do the dishes, but Gladys insisted on helping. Alice began collecting our plates as the women headed back to the kitchen.

"So, where are you three planning to stay tonight?" Berger asked.

"Under the great starry canopy," Tink pronounced, arching his arm overhead. "Where else?"

Berger chuckled. "I've slept in that hotel a time or two. The beds are awful hard."

"We've grown calluses on our calluses," I said.

"We have a nice hotel here in Elfrida."

"Hotels cost money," I said.

"I think I can arrange a room for the three of you tonight."

"That would be great!" Tink blurted.

His eagerness was almost embarrassing. "You don't have to . . ." I started, but Berger stopped me and said he wanted to do it.

Then a second knock came at the door.

"Evening, Marshal," a man said when Berger answered it.

"Evening, Irvin. Get a reply to that telegram?"

"Right here." He waved a paper. "And something else, too."

"Come inside."

The telegrapher started over the threshold, but when he saw Tink and me sitting there he hesitated. "Maybe I ought to show this to you out here on the porch."

A suspicious scowl moved across Berger's face. "All right." He took up a lamp, and they stepped outside.

"Wonder what that's about," Tink whispered worriedly.

"I don't know." I went to the window and peeked around the edge of the shade. Berger and Irvin were standing on the porch, peering at a telegram. Berger held the lamp high. A nervous knot had begun to tighten inside me, and I desperately wanted to hear what they were saying. I moved to another window that was open to a breeze but couldn't hear a thing.

Then I saw it. A speck of red over by the corner of the house. It brightened momentarily, and the next moment I smelled the smoke from one of Waldo's cocaine cigarettes. I backed away and returned to the table just as the door opened and Ed Berger came back inside the house.

Tink slanted a questioning eyebrow in my direction. I shrugged. Berger shut the door and came to the table. The marshal slid a sheet of paper at me while folding up a second sheet and shoving it into his vest pocket.

"Take a look at this."

"What's this?" I asked, trying not to let my nervousness show.

"Word on those yahoos who murdered Franklin. The one killed was called Kid Costello. Costello had made a reputation for himself down in El Paso. Sheriff Hackler says they haven't been able to learn who the others were. So there we have it. One dead outlaw and no leads on the others." A sudden frown tipped his mouth, and he shook his head. "That just don't seem right, does it?" he blurted angrily. Then he grimaced and his voice lost its edge. I saw that Ed Berger was a man used to the potholes in life's road. "Hackler says he's checking to see if there's any reward money on Costello. If there is, he says he'll hold it for you boys, for stopping Costello."

That sounded great, but I wasn't thinking so much of the possible reward money as I was the other telegram that he *didn't* show us. Maybe it was nothing at all, but when you hauled around a guilty conscious, everything looked suspicious.

Waldo strolled in a little while later, grinning

ear to ear and looking peacock pleased with himself. He always did after smoking one of those cigarettes—only more so tonight. I thought maybe he'd smoked two or three of 'em, but that wasn't it at all. And I didn't know what had pleased him so until later, when we were all finally alone in the hotel room that Marshal Berger had rented for us.

Waldo flopped onto one of the beds, stuck his hands behind his head, and grinned up at the ceiling.

"Okay, okay, so what got into you tonight?" I asked.

"Oh, not much. I just discovered something that will make us all rich!"

Tink had been prodding another bed, testing the springs. "I think I've heard that before." He lifted back the covers and checked the mattress for ticks.

"This time it's the real thing."

"Is it something to do with that telegram Berger got?" I opened the window and leaned out, relishing the cool night air. Down the street the Crystal Slipper was doing a brisk business; its piano music sounded inviting. I was thinking another beer would taste good.

"It is."

Douglas Hirt

I pulled back into the room. "It didn't have anything to do with . . . with us?"

"No."

I let out a sigh. "Thought for sure it was word of your breakout."

"You worry too much, Howie."

Tink punched up a pillow and stretched out. "So, what is it this time that's gonna make us rich?"

"Use that tone of voice with me and I'm not sure I want to tell you."

Tink gave a short laugh as he toed off his boots and they thumped to the floor. "Then don't tell me."

But Waldo couldn't keep it to himself. "I heard them talking, the marshal and that telegrapher. The telegram was from the railroad in Willcox. The Apache Mining Company is sending a payroll shipment through Elfrida Tuesday on its way down to Douglas. It's coming on a plain, ordinary supply wagon and no one is supposed to know about it, so they aren't expecting any trouble, but they wanted the marshal to be aware of it and to keep his eyes open for any strangers. Only two guards and the driver." Waldo grinned smugly at the ceiling. "*That's* what is gonna make us rich, Mr. Tinkerman."

Neither Tink nor I spoke right away. This was something different, something bigger and

166

bolder than we had ever attempted. I knew now why Waldo had been grinning all evening. A chill of excitement and fear skittered up my spine.

"How can we rob a mine payroll when there's gonna be guards? Armed guards!"

"Yeah." Tink sat up and swung his feet to the floor. "What do we do if they start to shoot at us?"

"We shoot back," Waldo said evenly, his dark eyes narrowing slightly.

"But someone might get hurt," Tink countered.

"If someone gets hurt, it will be them!" The sudden, hard edge in his voice was something I couldn't ever remember being there before. Waldo sat up suddenly and stared at us. "Listen, you two. We've been playing easy for over a year now and where has it gotten us? Nowhere! Now suddenly here is our big chance. The mother lode! We'll be sitting pretty if we can pull this one off. And we'll finally make people stand up and take notice to us."

"I don't particularly want people to take notice of me," I said.

Waldo's expression darkened.

Tink squirmed on the edge of the bed. "A man can end up dead shooting it out with armed guards."

"You scared?"

"Well, frankly, yeah, I am."

Waldo snorted. "Don't go soft on me now."

Tink shifted his view to the floor.

"Tink's right."

"Howie, I thought you'd be excited about this."

"Well . . . I am. Only, I don't see how we can pull it off without ending up full of holes."

"Let me worry about that."

"And even if we do pull it off, you can't go telling anyone that it was the Fritz Gang what done it," I continued.

"Why not?"

"Because one mention of the name Fritz and Marshal Berger is going to know exactly who done it. He knows you now. He knows all of us. He'll run us down and haul us back to that four-by-four jail of his."

Tink stood and paced a circle. "We'll be putting a rope around our necks if word ever gets out that it was the three of us that held up that payroll shipment."

Waldo's mouth tightened, disappointment showing on his face. "All right, so maybe we can't let on that it was the Fritz Gang that done it. That don't matter so long as we get the money. Afterward we'll have the cash to move on and pick up somewhere else where nobody knows us."

"All right," Tink said, "for the sake of argument, suppose we were to hold up that payroll. How do you see us going about it without, like Howie said, ending up full of holes?"

"That's easy. We get the drop on those guards before they know what's happening."

"Oh. That's so simple. I should have thought of it myself," Tink gibed.

"Shut that trap before I shut it for you."

Tink glared at him.

"He's right," I said, coming to Tink's defense. "What you're talking is crazy unless you got a plan. A very good plan."

"If you'd both just shut up long enough to listen, I'd tell you."

Tink and I bristled at his overbearing tone, but we bit back our words and nodded our heads. "All right," I said, "we'll listen. But it better be good."

Waldo sprang to his feet, nervous fingers shoving through his thick black hair. The light from our lamp reflected off his wide, earnest eyes, turning his face into a sculpture of sharp angles and shadowed planes.

"I've been thinking about it all evening. There's nothing to it. That road between Willcox and Douglas is a lonely stretch of nothing.

169

Douglas Hirt

We can surprise them anywhere along it—especially south of here. I spent some time in Douglas, remember? I know of a place where it winds through some narrows as it cuts along the eastern edge of the Pedrogosa Mountains. It used to be called—and still is sometimes— the Fronteras Road, 'cause back in the old days it was the way most folks took to go south of the border to Fronteras. It's still just as wild and just as empty as it was twenty years ago, in spite of all the new mines and towns springing up."

"That isn't a plan, Waldo," Tink chided, "it's a geography lesson."

Waldo scowled. "It could be," he said smugly. "Like I said, I know of this place."

"Yeah, like Napoleon knew Waterloo."

Waldo and Tink were feeding off of each other. Before it got out of hand, I stepped between them. "All right, so how do you figure we can get our hands on this payroll?"

He shot Tink a withering glance, then looked at me. "There's a place where the road narrows between some rocks. Just beyond that is a wide wash where there's a bridge. All we got to do is make that payroll wagon leave the road, then stop it and jump the guards before they know what happened."

Tink started to object, but I waved him back and asked the question I knew was on his mind.

170

"Two problems, Waldo. First, how do we divert the wagon? And second, how do we stop it once we do?"

"I got that all figured out, Howie," he said confidently. "All we got to do is pick up a few supplies Monday morning before we leave here."

Tink tried again. I was one step ahead of him. "What sort of supplies?"

"Oh, just a few things. A couple rolls of rope, some red cloth, a shotgun . . . and, oh yeah, a few dozen sticks of dynamite."

"Dynamite!" Tink yelped.

"I told you. I got a plan."

Chapter Thirteen

Marshal Berger shook our hands and Alice gave each of us a hug.

"Will I ever see you again?" she asked.

"Sure you will," I said. "We'll stop by sometime and see how you are getting along."

"Thanks for all that you have done," Berger said. "We'll be leaving in the morning to take care of Franklin's business and see to the grave. Gladys needs to say her good-byes."

"Yes, thank you for all you have done." Gladys gave us a thin smile and took our hands in a light grip. She was looking better. Sad, of course, but the tears had stopped. She put a hand on Alice's shoulder, and the three of them stood there on the front porch as we rode away from the house.

172

In town, we stopped by the big warehouse and bought some dynamite and a couple coils of heavy rope. Waldo had explained it to us the night before, but I was skeptical. It was a bolder scheme than we had ever attempted before, but if it worked we'd three be set up for a good long time. If it didn't . . . I shivered, not wanting to go down that path.

Our next stop was the hardware store, where Waldo looked over the shotguns and handed over most of what little money we had left for a used Hopkins & Allen and a box of twelve-gauge shells. Finally we stopped by a Whorley's general mercantile and spent our last few pennies on a yard of red cloth, a couple sheets of cardboard, and a red crayon. We shoved all this into our saddlebags, putting the dynamite and fuse into Waldo's and the box of blasting caps into mine.

On our way out of town Waldo drew up and stopped in the middle of the street to consider the Crystal Slipper Saloon.

"What's wrong?" I asked.

"I was just thinking that someday I might settle down and buy me a place like that."

I laughed. "You mean you're taking seriously that line you fed to Marshal Berger—about looking for a business to buy?"

A faint smile touched Waldo's lips. "Why

not?" he jutted his chin at the saloon. "A man who owned that would be a man of influence in a town like this." He looked around, as if appraising Elfrida with a fresh eye, and nodded his head, then clucked his horse onward.

We left Elfrida behind us and took the old Fronteras Road south toward Douglas.

I was mighty nervous, and sitting around doing nothing but waiting only made it worse. Tink was nervous too, though he didn't say it in words. When his humor became darker and he no longer laughed at his own jokes, then you knew he was fretting mighty heavily about something.

"How long has he been gone?" Tink asked finally.

I was crouched in the shade beneath the bridge, listening to the trickle of water nearby. Tink had been stalking up and down the ravine for the last half hour, kicking dirt over the rope we'd laid out earlier, making sure none of the red flags showed.

I shrugged. "Couple hours."

Tink came over and splashed water onto his face. From where I was hunkered under the crossbeams, I could look straight up at the bundles of dynamite packed alongside the timbers. Between them, short fuses all ran together into a single main line that hung down near my right shoulder.

Squinting out into the glaring light, I studied the tracks our horses had made. We'd spent an hour riding back and forth between the two low banks of the ravine to make it look as if a lot of folks had taken that route. We wanted it to appear a well-used detour—and it did.

"Should we do it?" Tink swept off his hat and swiped the sweat from his forehead.

"I reckon. Waldo wanted the job done by the time he got back."

Tink took a match from his shirt pocket. "You want to do the honor, or should I?"

"You do it. Just let me give the road a final check. Wouldn't want to find someone crossing over about the time all that dynamite blows." I levered my hat onto my head and scooted out into the heat. Scrambling up the side of the ravine, I checked the road in each direction. It was empty as a church pew on Monday morning. "All clear!"

Tink struck the patch and put it to the fuse. Then we scrambled out of there and took the horses around to the back side of a low intervening hill to wait.

The explosion rocked the air, and when the dust had settled half that bridge lay on its side with planks twisted every which way.

175

"No wagon is going over that," Tink observed with a satisfied note in his voice.

"Nope. Let's finish up now." We strung a rope across the road on both sides of the bridge and hung out our pieces of cardboard.

Bridge out. I'd scrawled the words with the crayon and drawn a big red arrow pointing down the slope where we'd laid our false trail. The wind quickly dispersed the smoke and dust and most of the remaining odor of dynamite. No one came along to investigate the explosion, and that was how we hoped it would be. About an hour later, pounding hoofbeats brought us to our feet.

A horse galloped into view, and a few moments later Waldo reined to a stop. "They're coming!" He swung off the saddle and quickly led the lathered horse out of sight behind the low hill.

"How far?" I asked.

"I rode pretty hard to give us time to get ready. They're about an hour behind me. I see you got the bridge ready."

"Probably went a little overboard on the dynamite." Tink nodded at the twisted shape crumpled in the middle of the ravine.

"It'll serve our purpose," Waldo replied. "You two know what to do?"

"I think so. Once we've stopped them in the

ravine, Tink and I rush them from behind. You'll come down from over there. If we're lucky, no one will start shooting."

"And if we're not lucky?" Tink cast a questioning glance at Waldo.

"Then you better be prepared to defend yourselves. And try to remember what I've taught you. It's a sure bet that those guards will be shooting fast."

"But fast isn't always the best," I reminded Waldo, repeating the advice he'd often given to us.

"That's right, Howie. Keep it in mind. It's not how fast you clear leather, but how straight you shoot."

It all sounded so right, so easy. Yet if shooting ever did get started, I doubted I'd be able to remain cool enough to remember any of what Waldo had tried to drum into our heads.

"Let's check it out one last time," Waldo said.

We strolled down into the wide gravelly bottom and walked along the route of the rope that we'd buried in the hot sand. On the other side of the wash, the rope snaked over the thick limb of an old cottonwood tree, then folded down the other side. There we'd tied it to a heavy length of gnarled driftwood propped up on a stick. A second rope was fastened to the stick so that it could be easily yanked away by a man on horseback. It all looked okay. Satisfied that everything was going to work according to plan, we went back to our horses and moved to our stations.

Tink and I hid behind the hill. Waldo had given me the shotgun. "A big old scattergun like this will make any sane man think twice about going for his gun," he had said. He went across the way to the deadfall. From where we waited, Waldo was completely out of sight.

"I sure hope this works," I said as we sat there in the sun on our horses.

"You nervous?"

"Me? Nervous? Hah! . . . I'm terrified."

"Yeah, so's this hombre." Tink grinned.

"You'd think it would get easier."

"Only if you're cut out for this line of work."

I grimaced. "Maybe I'm not cut out for it, Tink."

"You aren't. And neither am I."

"I thought it would be great fun and we'd make lots of money, or so Waldo told us," I said. "Well, we haven't made much of anything this last year."

"That's the straight of it." Tink suddenly cocked his head to one side, listening. "Hear that?"

"A wagon's coming." My chest tightened. Hurriedly I wiped the sweat from my hands, then gripped that shotgun until my knuckles showed white. "Here we go," I whispered.

"Yep." Tink fixed his bandanna over his face. I did too.

The wagon drew nearer, and I caught a glimpse of it from where we hid. "Apache Mining Co." was painted in big yellow letters across the side of the wagon box, which was otherwise covered in a bulky tarp. Behind it was a tethered horse. Two men rode on the seat, and a third was following alongside on horseback.

They slowed, then drew to a halt. "What's this?" one of them asked.

The man on horseback rode forward and peered at the bridge. "Wonder what happened here. Something sure made a mess of this bridge." He glanced at our signs, then turned toward the slope where we'd laid down all those tracks. "Looks like we're gonna have to take it down here."

"Kinda steep," the driver said.

"Back it up and let's give it a try," the rider replied.

The driver clucked to his horses and eased back on the reins, running the wagon to the rear a few dozen feet, then turning it to the slope.

"Take it easy," warned the passenger as he gripped the iron handhold. The wagon lurched on its heavy springs while the driver rode the brake. It swayed, then skidded to a stop at the bottom of the ravine.

"Almost lost it." The driver shook his head. "Hope they get that bridge fixed before our next run." He clucked at the team and got them moving toward the other side.

I caught my breath.

Tink was staring, hardly breathing either. "Right . . . about . . . now," he whispered.

There was a sharp crack. The buried rope snapped up, sending a shower of sand skyward. Instantly, dozens of red flags fluttered across the ravine. The startled horses skittered sideways while the driver fought the reins.

"Now!" Tink and I burst from cover, our guns ready. Before any of them knew what had happened, we had them covered.

"Don't try it!" I shifted the muzzle of the shotgun toward one of the riders, who had started for his gun. His hand hesitated, then backed away from the holster, and he reached for the sky.

"What's going on here?" the passenger growled.

My heart had climbed clear into my throat, and suddenly I couldn't say another word. Luckily, the next instant Waldo appeared from behind the cottonwood tree and rode in among us.

"You're carrying payroll. I want it," he said, showing them the muzzle of his revolver.

"Payroll? No, you got it all wrong, mister. Just got regular supplies here, that's all." The driver's eyes darted between us. "Steel cable and grease and shovels. Stuff like that. You can take a look if you want."

"I happen to know better," Waldo said evenly. "Hand it over or I start shooting."

My view snapped around to Waldo. I'd never heard him give that kind of threat before, and I crossed my fingers that none of these men would call his bluff. If they did, we'd have to make tracks out of here mighty quick.

There was a long silence as the three of them exchanged glances. I was hardly breathing. A strange electricity had filled the air all around us. I knew what those glances meant, but I didn't want to believe it. They weren't going to hand over the money! They were thinking the same thing. Waldo was running a bluff, and one of them was about to call it.

A glance at Tink told me he was feeling it too. Instinctively, I backed my horse a couple steps. Waldo's hard eyes narrowed, and I saw his jaw take a firm set beneath the bandanna he wore.

All at once the man on horseback had a gun in his hand. It wasn't his revolver, but a tiny Remington derringer that he'd pulled from his sleeve. In a flash he swung the pistol at Waldo, and it cracked like a firecracker.

Waldo's horse reared and whinnied, and then everything was in motion, with everyone shooting at everyone else—everyone but me and Tink, that is. We'd both gone stiff as dead men. Our horses were bucking and fighting their bits, and I had all I could do just to keep in the saddle and duck my head . . . as if that would do one bit of good against a bullet.

As suddenly as it had begun, the shooting stopped. I settled my horse and checked myself all over for blood. There wasn't any. Waldo was still atop his horse, looking ghostlike through the cloud of gun smoke that enveloped him. One man was sprawled on the ground, and two more were slumped over on the wagon seat.

I gave a shiver, leaped to the ground, and went to the man on the ground. "He's dead!" The little pistol was still in his fingers. I pried it loose and saw that he'd only managed to fire one of the barrels. I dropped the derringer into my pocket.

"This one is still alive," Tink said of the driver after giving the two on the wagon a quick check.

We lifted him down to the shady side of the wagon and took off his shirt. Waldo's bullet had punched a hole clear through his bacon and busted one of his lower ribs. Waldo strode over as we worked to stop the flow.

"Thanks for the help, *partners!*" he growled.

"You killed two of them!" I said, fetching my canteen. I gave the man a drink and he started to come around.

"Can't waste time over this one," Waldo said as he went around to the back of the wagon and sliced open the tarp with a knife.

"Well, we can't let him bleed to death," Tink said.

"Why not?" There was an icy note in Waldo's voice. He rummaged through the supplies. It was pretty much as the man had said. Just supplies. Things a mine might use on a regular basis.

"Damn!" Waldo stalked around the wagon and leaned low toward the wounded man. "Where is it?" His revolver leaped to his hand. "Tell me or I'll finish it here and now."

He was in shock, but his eyes widened quickly when Waldo's gun leveled at his nose. "Under seat. False bottom."

Waldo found the small iron chest. It was heavy for its size, and he hauled it to the ground. He fired at the lock, and the bullet zinged off the hardened steel as if it had been made of rubber instead of lead. Waldo cursed again.

"Let's get out of here before someone comes along," he ordered. "Now!" he barked.

Douglas Hirt

We'd done what we could for the man. "Someone will be along soon," I told him, leaving my canteen with him.

The man only nodded, still dazed. I put his hand on the cloth that we'd wadded up against the bullet hole. He had the strength to hold it in place.

Waldo nodded at the box. I took hold of one of the iron handles and he the other. Together we carried it to our horses and, keeping the heavy box between us, mounted up. Side by side, we rode away from there, toward the Pedrogosa Mountains.

Chapter Fourteen

We kept to a rocky ridge of land where our tracks would be difficult to decipher. It was difficult going, especially trying to hold a heavy cash box between two riders.

I was thinking about those two dead men behind us, and the wounded fellow we had left alone; feeling pretty miserable and down, and wondering how we'd ever come so far as to kill for money. I wondered about Waldo, too. He'd changed since we first began riding together. This fire within him to have a reputation and a name had begun to burn out of control. A cold finger ran up my spine. In the beginning it was about excitement, about finding my own way in the world. It was about Pa, too, I think, and what he stood for and what I stood for. Now I had my own way, my own life, and looking over it, I wasn't very happy with what I had become.

Tink scouted ahead for the best trail, and after about an hour were dropped into a little canyon that meandered back into the hills, narrowing as it went until it came to an end.

"Nobody will track us back here," Waldo said, going around to examine his horse.

Tink stepped off his horse and led it into the shade of the tall walls.

I handed my reins over to Tink and helped steady Waldo's mount. We'd seen blood on its neck as we rode. "How bad is it?"

"It's stopped bleeding." Waldo ran a hand along the horse's neck, gently probing with a finger. "There," he said, feeling the lump beneath the skin. "Buried itself in heavy muscle. That bullet would have been in me if it wasn't for this old fellow getting in the way." He stroked the horse's thick neck and gave him an affectionate scratch behind the ears. "Lucky for you that pip-squeak of a gun doesn't pack much of a wallop, ain't that right?"

"It should be cut out."

"We'll have to find someone who can do it," Waldo agreed. "Maybe next town we come to."

"How we going to open that box?" Tink asked.

Waldo and I turned to consider the iron chest we'd dropped to the ground. He picked it up and hauled it a hundred feet or so down the canyon and fired at the lock four or five times. I tried with my revolver too, but all we succeeded in doing was ricocheting a lot of lead.

"It don't want to open," I said. "Ain't that the hell of it? We stole the box but can't get the money inside."

"We'll get it," Waldo said with determination.

"If there was only some way to cut that hasp," I thought aloud.

"I know." Waldo examined the iron loop where the lock passed thought it. "Howie, I've got a file in my saddlebags. Bring it to me."

I didn't like being ordered around, but I went for it anyway. The file was where he said it would be . . . and something else too. At the bottom of one of the saddlebags was a paisley coin purse. Mr. Deavers's coin purse! I'd forgotten all about it. Waldo had never showed it since way back when we'd spent all the money. I'd thought he'd thrown it away a year before. But there it was. And it was packed full!

I opened it and saw the gleam of gold. I frowned, and glanced at Waldo. He was still peering at that chest. I took the pouch and swung by where Tink sat in the shade, giving him a warning look and dropping it into his hand. I could tell by his sudden, surprised ex-

187

pression that he was thinking the same thing as me.

"Here you go," I said to Waldo, giving him the file. He dragged the chest into the shade and began working at the hasp. We took turns for the next hour until finally we cut through it on one side. Using the blade of his knife, Waldo pried the metal back and the padlock fell free. Greedily, he hauled out two sacks. His fingers flew over the knots, undoing them, and the glittering gold coins spilled into the empty chest.

Tink's eyes rounded.

Waldo scooped up a double handful of coins and let them dribble through his fingers. "Bonanza!"

I'd never seen so much money in my life. Waldo let out a laugh when he saw my expression. "You're catching flies, Howie."

I cranked my jaw back together. "Must be ten thousand dollars there!"

"It will be a long while before we run out of money again," Waldo declared.

My euphoria vanished. "Yeah. A long time." My suddenly flat tone made him look up.

"What is it?" he asked warily, sensing the change that had come over me. He glanced at Tink, who was frowning—something rarer than snow in this part of the country. Waldo's shoulders tensed as he stood and faced us like a man suddenly backed into a corner. "If you're thinking of taking it all for yourself, well, don't even try it." His hand lowered to his side, and I knew that if we spooked him, if he went for it, Tink and I were dead men.

"We aren't going to take but what belongs to us, Waldo," I said.

"Then what is it?"

I nodded toward Tink. His hand came from his pocket holding Deaver's coin purse. He opened it and spilled the money at Waldo's feet. "You've been holding out on us, Waldo," he said. "I counted it. There's over two hundred dollars."

"It's no wonder we're always broke, with you keeping part of it back for yourself," I added.

We'd caught him off guard, but he recovered in a flash. "Oh, is that what this is all about?" Waldo laughed. "All right, so I was keeping some back. I was just holding it for emergencies. I wasn't keeping it for myself."

I said, "You might have been able to convince us of that a year ago, Waldo, but not now."

He shrugged. "So take the money. We have so much now, that little bit ain't gonna mean nothing."

"That's not the point," Tink said, tossing the paisley pouch onto the pile of coins.

189

"What *is* the point?" Waldo's voice hardened, that put-on lightness disappearing.

"We were partners. We trusted you, and all the while you were stealing from us."

"There is no honor among thieves, Tink. I thought you'd figured that out by now."

With the edge of my boot, I shoved the money alongside the sack of gold coins that hadn't yet been opened. "Let's divide it up."

"Sure. We'll divide it up," Waldo said.

That took most of the next hour while the sun moved lower in the sky, taking the edge off the heat down in that narrow ravine. When it was all said and done with, we each had about nine thousand dollars: what a man might earn in a lifetime of working in the mines, I calculated—at least a miner's lifetime. I bundled it up in one of the canvas sacks and Tink put his share into the other.

I put the gold into my saddlebags and mounted up.

"Where are you going?"

"Leaving."

"Why? Because of that little thing about the money? Grow up, Howie."

"That's only part of it, Waldo. You've changed. You didn't have to kill those men back there. It was stupid and risky taking on an armed payroll shipment. We both told you so.

190

But you have this thing in your head about making a name for yourself. It's so filled you up that I think you were looking for an excuse to kill them. Well, if it ever gets out who pulled this one off, you will have made a big name for yourself, all right. Only, I don't want to be a part of it. I'm leaving, Waldo. I don't need you anymore, and I don't need to go on robbing folks, either. You're telling me to grow up? That's exactly what I'm doing. See you around."

I turned my horse away from him and out the corner of my eye saw Tink heading for his.

"Where are you going?" Waldo asked Tink.

"I'm pulling out with Howie. He's right. After today we're all going to be in big trouble if anyone finds out. Besides, I know Howie ain't going to steal nothing from me. Adios, Waldo."

"You guys are making a big mistake," he called after us.

"It wouldn't be the first time," Tink hooted, lifting an arm in a parting wave.

"You can't just walk out on me like this! You two will be sorry, I promise you!"

I didn't look back. Far as I was concerned, I was through with Waldo Fritz. A big weight lifted from my shoulders as we wound our way out of that tight ravine, but I was still troubled when I thought of those two men, dead back on the Fronteras Road. I wondered how long it was going to take to forget that—or if I ever would. Tink and I didn't say a word until we finally emerged at the mouth of that canyon and I reined to a stop.

"Thanks for coming along," I said.

Tink grinned. "Someone's got to look after you. Already told you that's my job. After all, I'm a whole year older than you, Howie." He laughed.

"Good to hear you laugh. You haven't been doing much of that lately."

"Yeah, well, that's past. We're starting out new, Howie."

"Sounds good." I drew the cooling air deep into my lungs and felt a little better.

"So what now, partner, since it's just you and me?"

I thought a moment. "We finally got us money. I say we go find us that good town you keep looking for."

"Hallelujah!" Tink tossed his hat high in the air and went galloping after it. It reminded me of the day we left Bisbee. I hoped this next year would prove better than the one just gone by. Putting heels to my horse, I gave a shout and raced after him.

We headed east, moving deeper into the Pedrogosa Mountains. I didn't know about Tink, but I was trying to put Elfrida and the past far behind me. I was looking forward to finally finding that good town that Tink was always searching for. Then maybe, once enough time had gone by, I could go home again and see my family.

For some reason that was suddenly more important to me than it had been for a good long time.

193

Chapter Fifteen

Devil's Falls, Arizona

We drew rein and sat there studying the weathered sign. Beyond it, a row of clapboard buildings staggered along this wide spot in the road. We were somewhere between San Carlos and Florence, and that was all I knew. This was mining country again, but we were a good piece north of where we'd left Waldo. That had been nearly three months before, past the hot part of the summer. We were looking forward to the coming fall.

Tink and I figured it was safer to stay on the move and away from the bigger towns until memory of the robbery, which had made big news all around, faded from most folks' minds.

I'm sure Waldo had been pleased, especially with his picture finally showing up in the papers and on a Wanted poster. They'd drawn him with the mask on, of course, but the eyes were about right, and so were the sharp cheekbones, dark brows, and that black hat he wore. I recognized him right off, but then, I knew Waldo. To someone who hadn't ever seen him before, the artist's sketch was just that, a sketch, and probably no one would recognize Waldo behind it. Thankfully, neither Tink's nor my face had made it onto a poster. There had only been mention of two others who had been involved, and no names.

Just the same, we fought shy of any town where there might be a sitting sheriff, or where we saw telegraph and telephone wires strung out. We stuck close to the high country—which meant mining camps—and that's how we found ourselves at Devil's Falls, near the southern foot of the Superstition Mountains.

"What do you think?" I asked.

"Looks like a good town—from here," Tink allowed with little enthusiasm. Lately we'd considered and rejected a dozen prospective "good towns," and our enthusiasm was a little peaked.

I didn't pay much attention to the buildings as we rode past them into town. They were pretty much the same in every hamlet we hit.

After all, folks everywhere needed food and clothes and tools and drugs, a place to keep their money, and another place to wet their whistles. It was the latter that I was looking for. It had been a good long while since we'd had us a beer or any grub that didn't come out of our own pans, and Tink and me had developed a mighty thirst.

"There," Tink said, angling his horse across the hard-baked street toward a hitching rail. A sign above the porch that wrapped around two sides of the building said "Whipple Johnson Saloon." We found some shade on the east side of the saloon and tied our horses near a scum-covered trough. The horses didn't seem to mind the scum, nudging it aside to get at the clearer water beneath.

We took our saddlebags with us. We never went far from them these days. Though we looked like two dirt-poor drifters, all the gold we carried with us made us rich men.

It was cool inside. We strode to the bar, allowing our eyes to get used to the muted light. The bartender was sitting at a table with a couple of men and came over when he saw us.

"Strangers in town," he said with a light-hearted lilt and a friendly crinkle about his eyes. "Just get in?"

"This is our first stop," I said.

A Good Town

"Usually is for most men off a dry and dusty road." He looked us up and down. "Like you two. What will it be?"

We ordered beers. He drew them from a barrel and told us the first drink for strangers was on the house.

"Thank you!" Tink saluted him with the mug.

The man grinned and went back to his friends. We took a table, and someone across the room glanced up, grinned, and gave us a small wave.

I waved back.

"Folks seem mighty friendly here in Devil's Falls," Tink said.

"Maybe they don't get many strangers through."

"Maybe. I didn't see any mines when we rode in. Wonder what men do here."

I shrugged. "Appears a pretty lazy place."

"Might be a good town to stay with."

"For a while. Until it proves not to be. But we still have to find a way to make a living. We may be carrying around a good amount of money"— I patted my saddlebag—"but it isn't going to last forever."

"We could deposit it for interest," Tink suggested.

"What do banks give nowadays?"

"I've heard some as high as two percent," he said.

I did the numbers in my head. "That amounts to about a hundred and eighty dollars a year apiece. Can't hardly live on that."

Tink frowned. "Reckon you're right. We need to get a job or live off our principal. Once that's gone, we're right back where we started."

I grinned. "Yeah, but think of all that rich living. It's going to take a lot of years to go through nine thousand dollars."

He grinned, too, and we clinked our mugs together and turned them up toward the ceiling until we could see the old chandelier through the thick bottom.

"Ready for another?" the bartender asked from the table where he sat chatting with his friends.

"Another!" Tink declared, putting the mug down with a bang.

The man brought two more beers over and collected our money. We asked him what folks did here in Devil's Falls to make a dollar.

"Well . . ." He drew the word out, considering. "Some haul freight up from Florence. Some haul it down to Florence. Then some tend stores . . . and others tend saloons." He laughed, his thick cheeks puffing up and his eyes narrowing. "There's Ben Wilson over at the livery who sells mules to the prospectors. Lots of prospectors about. Tales of hidden gold mines bring 'em to these mountains in droves. And then there's Orin Whal, who farms squash and frijoles in the valley, and runs the greengrocer's shop. Kerwin over there," the bartender jabbed a thumb at one of the men he'd been talking to at the table, "he runs an assay office and sells mining supplies. Then we have us a banker, a shoemaker, a blacksmith, even a sawbones"—he gave us a sudden wink—"and we provide a few other services. So I guess you can say folks here in Devil's Falls do a little bit of everything. Why do you ask?"

In spite of its isolation, which I found much to my liking at the moment, Devil's Falls seemed to have everything a man might need to make him comfortable. "Me and my friend, we're kinda looking for a place to knock off the trail dust and settle down in for a while."

"Been looking for a good town," Tink said.

"Devils Falls is a pretty good town," he allowed. "By the way, my name is Hector Johnson." He stuck out a big, fleshy hand. It was warm and sweaty, and I slyly wiped my hand on my britches after shaking it.

"I'm Howard Blake, and this here is my partner, Dobie Tinkerman. But we go by Howie and

Tink. If you're Mr. Johnson, where's Mr. Whipple?"

He laughed. "You must have read the sign out front. Whipple, he sold out to me about two years ago. Went out west somewhere. Utah, or Nevada. I don't know where he finally ended up. I've been meaning to have that shingle changed, but never got around to it." He grinned. "Come on over and join us. We're just jawing away the afternoon. Business usually doesn't pick up around here until June or July." He laughed, and we picked up our mugs and moved over to their table.

Johnson introduced us to his friends. Kerwin Mattalino, the assayer whom Johnson had already mentioned, was a stout fellow with a salt-and-pepper beard and blue eyes. Beside him sat Phillip Swan, a thin, little man with long fingers and small, round spectacles perched atop a slender nose. Swan smiled a lot but didn't say much. Johnson said he ran some sort of service business, but was kinda vague as to what sort of services. The third man was a young fellow, about our own age, with a high twittering laugh and a splotchy brown beard that looked about the way Tink's had a year before. Tink had become right proud of his beard now. I still couldn't grow one and didn't even try. They simply called the kid Woody. He was a cook at the

Hildebrandt Café, a couple of doors up the street.

"Why do you call your town Devil's Falls?" Tink asked.

"Because of the waterfall," Mattalino said.

"You have a waterfall here?" There was surprise in my voice. The place looked drier than an old chicken bone.

"Oh, sure," Johnson led off. "And it's a dandy when it's running. Course, this time of year there ain't so much as a trickle. But come spring, it's a regular Niagara." He chuckled.

"It's just north of town," Swan added in a small, high voice.

"We'll have to take a look," Tink said, and followed it with a long drink from his mug.

I was feeling relaxed, but I didn't want to get too relaxed. I set my saddlebags on the floor under the table and caught them between my feet for safekeeping. Johnson disappeared into a back room and came back a few minutes later with a platter of sandwiches. Tink and I dove into those like men escaping a sinking ship. Then we had another beer. Some men came in and some left, but Tink and me, we were glued there. The company was amiable, and the conversation shifted around with no particular goal in sight.

"What do you two have in mind to do, if you

decide to stay here?" Swan asked us at one point.

"Do?" I slurred, and grinned, thinking that we'd probably end up robbing a few stores. I was still sober enough to mind my tongue, but my brain wasn't clicking over too quickly, so I stole a line from right out of Waldo's book. "Maybe Tink and me, we'll buy us a business— or start one. Ain't that right, Tink?"

Tink nodded as he grabbed for his beer mug, nearly missing the handle.

"Buying or starting a business takes capital," Swan advised in a professional sort of way, as if he knew about such things.

"That's no problem," Tink said recklessly. He started to reach for the saddlebags at his feet, but I shot him a narrow glance. He caught himself, straightened up quickly, and added, "That is, me and Howie, we aren't afraid of hard work to earn what we need."

I winced. If that was true, I'd still be back in Bisbee following in Pa's footsteps.

"A man willing to work hard can accomplish most anything," Mattalino commented. He stroked his beard in a contemplative manner, as if reflecting on something.

"How about another beer?" Johnson prodded.

Tink was up for it, but I figured we'd had

enough. "I think Tink and me might want to wander around and look the town over a bit."

Tink was about to object, but another warning glance silenced him. We all shook hands and said how we were looking forward to getting together again, then staggered outside into the late-noon glare.

"What was that all about?" Tink groused once out of earshot.

"You didn't need another beer. You almost spilled the beans about our money."

He gave a lame smile. "Yeah, guess you're right, Howie. I'm sorry."

"That's all right. No harm was done." We'd begun to walk, and I was taking notice this time of the buildings and the people around me. Devil's Falls was looking more and more appealing, especially since I had just spied a couple pretty gals who appeared young and unattached.

Tink must have been reading my thoughts. "This seems like a good town, Howie, don't you think?"

I nodded as my eye caught the shapely curves of another comely girl across the street. "Maybe we've found it after all." I stubbed my toe on a board and almost fell. My head was swimming, and Tink giggled.

"You're drunk."

"Am not," I shot back a bit too quickly, concentrating on walking a straight line and looking stone sober.

"Now you're walking like you sat down on a stick," he chided.

"Am not." I wasn't being too clever with my replies.

We tied our saddlebags back onto our horses and led them along the street. I was looking for that waterfall, figuring it had to be over where a cliff was just visible, past an apothecary shop and a small building advertising guns and barbed wire. "Over there."

"Over there what?" Tink asked.

"That must be where the waterfall is. Let's take a look."

"But it's dry this time of year," he protested. "I need to take a leak."

"Yeah, me too. There'll be a place over by the falls." I angled us toward the cliffs, and soon we were out of town. The place was a good four or five hundred feet beyond the last of the buildings—a row of tiny tinderbox shacks, each the same, with frilly curtains in the windows and some with flowers in pots out in front by the door.

"Those ain't hardly big enough for but a single bed," Tink observed. And just then a woman stuck her head outside the window and waved.

She had that same look in her eyes that I recalled seeing on some of the female faces back in Bisbee that night we all had gone down to Brewery Gulch.

"Mighty friendly people here in Devil's Falls," I reiterated. "Have you noticed all the women?"

"What women?"

"Tink, you really have had too much to drink. This town is just full of the sweetest-looking little fillies I'd ever seen in one place."

"Are you telling it straight?"

"Sure am."

Tink glanced over his shoulder, up the road into Devil's Falls. "In that case, this really is a good town. I'm for staying."

"Over there," I said, pointing.

"Huh?"

"The falls."

"Oh."

We plodded on toward the sheer cliff that loomed ahead, and stood there gawking. A rock ledge soared high overhead, worn smooth and rounded at the lip, streaked white in places as if a flock of big birds had spent some time roosting up there. It was most of a hundred feet high, and right below was the splash pool, only there wasn't any water in it today. It was just a big, deep sandbox, with rocks and gnarled wood strewn about. Some pretty big rocks were scattered about like half-buried marbles. A dry riverbed, lined with cottonwood trees, ran off to the south.

"This oughta be something to see come spring. Heh, Howie?" Tink tilted his head way back.

We tied our horses to a tree and staggered down into the parched pit. In the shade of the rock wall, we sat on a rock and looked around. I couldn't look up for very long. It made my head swim and my stomach go queasy. I tried to remember how many beers I'd had, and couldn't.

We were sitting there, craning our necks and exercising our eyeballs, when four men rode up. I recognized the little one called Swan and the stout one na med Mattalino, but the other two were strangers. They dismounted and tied their animals with ours, then Mattalino went around to his saddlebags and removed something from them. I couldn't tell what it was right off, and I was more curious than wary, which goes to show I'd had too much beer.

"What's this about?" Tink whispered as they strolled over. There was a note of concern in his voice, and that made me start to worry as we sat there watching them approach.

"Hello," I said.

"Hello again," Mattalino said with a wide

smile. Then he held up a bottle of whiskey. "Fancy meeting you two down here. Me and my friends, we're about to spend the evening here with our good friend, John Barleycorn. Mind if we join you?"

"Pull up a rock," Tink said.

Mattalino made the introductions, but I don't remember their names. They were an amiable bunch, easygoing, and mostly they complained about the heat, and the government, and wondered if Arizona was ever going to be admitted into statehood.

"Here, have a pull," Mattalino offered, passing the bottle to Tink and me. Swan tittered as if he'd already had too many pulls at it, and the others insisted. I knew I didn't need it, but Tink was eager to join in and I didn't want to spoil the party. I recalled my last encounter with whiskey and was careful not to repeat the disaster.

The bottle made the rounds and came back to me again. Its stinging venom had been neutralized by the time I'd had three or four swallows.

One fellow said he knew of a building for sale that was located in a prime spot. He'd put in a good word to the owner for us. The other offered to help us get it spruced up for business since he was a carpenter by trade and had experience in this field.

Swan just tittered and grinned, and as usual didn't say much.

I was impressed with the downright friendliness of everyone we'd met so far in Devil's Falls. And as we lazied around, enjoying each other's company and the whiskey, I knew that we'd finally found Tink's good town.

Chapter Sixteen

When I woke up the next morning, an elephant was sitting on my head with his tail stuck in my mouth. I tried to open my eyes, but the glaring morning sun drove spikes into them, nailing them shut. I groaned a low, grating grunt—the only sound my throat seemed capable of producing right then. I squirmed where I lay, only vaguely aware of the pain in my shoulders, back, and hips.

I groaned again and tried to spit out the elephant's tail, only to discover it was my own tongue. Reluctantly, painfully, I sat up and leaned against one of those boulders. The morning air was tainted with the odor of whiskey from my own breath, and from the nauseating stench of vomit nearby. I'd heaved my guts sometime during the night, still tasted it, and fought back a sudden urge to do so again.

I shaded my eyes, and everything was out of focus at first. Slowly it sharpened up. I was still in that dry streambed, and each sharp rock strewn about had left its mark on me during the night. I didn't see Mattalino or Swan, or the other two men. They must have left sometime during the night. Searching around some, I discovered Tink sprawled next to the cliff, that empty whiskey bottle still clutched in his lifeless fist.

"Tink," I croaked, suddenly craving water. I staggered to my feet and stepped a crooked path to Tink. Here and there were drying patches of vomit, seething with flies. The sight churned my stomach. I looked away and willed myself not to throw up again.

"Tink?" I collapsed to my knees and gave him a shake. He moaned in his sleep. The odor of whiskey about him was too much for me, and I wheeled away and emptied my stomach again. Tink squirmed, then rolled over and sat up. Dried vomit caked the front of his shirt. We both looked horrible, and smelled even worse.

"Water," he moaned, working his cracked lips as if munching on a piece of that same elephant's tail. I needed to rinse my mouth too, so I said I'd get the canteen and started for our horses, each step a jarring hammer blow to my head. I reached the animals, leaned a moment on my saddle, then slung a canteen over my shoulder and grabbed for the towel I keep in my saddlebags. I was surprised to discover that the buckles to the bags had already been loosed. But I didn't think anything of it until I opened the flap. . . .

It's truly amazing how fast sobriety can return to a man.

I checked the other side, then checked Tink's horse. The gold was gone. All of it.

The saloon was mostly empty this time of the morning. Hector Johnson flashed us one of his friendly smiles. "Howie, Tink. Boy, you two look horrible." He fanned a hand in front of his nose. "Ugh! I'm afraid I'm going to have to ask you two gentlemen to leave until you've had a bath and wash your clothes."

"Where are they?" I demanded.

"They?"

"Swan and Mattalino, and their friends."

Johnson shrugged. "Have no idea."

"Where do they live?" Tink growled. "The sonsuvabitches stole our gold last light!"

"That's a mighty serious accusation," Johnson said, losing the smile.

"Taking our gold is serious business," I shot

back. "Now, tell me where they can be found!"

"I'm not sure you two really want to go after them." Johnson's tone was suddenly heavy with warning.

"You got a sheriff in this town?" Tink demanded.

"No, but there's one over at Riverside on the Cottonwood Road."

"Then he's the man we'll be talking to."

"You might be making big trouble for yourself," Johnson said.

"Why? Because you're in with them thieves?"

His face hardened. "I just wouldn't go poking my nose where it doesn't belong."

I glanced at Tink. "Let's go find that sheriff." He nodded, and we started for the door.

Johnson said offhandedly, "Say, you two wouldn't know anything about that big payroll heist from the Apache Mining Company a few months back, would you?"

His words stopped us in our tracks. My heart quickened, and I turned cautiously to see the bartender grinning. I'd forgotten that we'd kept the gold in the canvas sacks with "Apache Mining Co." stenciled in black across them.

"No, no—don't know anything about that."

Tink's eyes, bloodshot as they were, were suddenly showing considerable white. "What makes you ask?"

He shrugged those meaty shoulders. "Just wondering. You two said you moved around a lot. Thought you might of had word on it. Figured if you did, when you went for the sheriff over at Riverside, you might be able to give him a lead as to the whereabouts of those low-down thieving murderers who killed two men and left another, wounded and bleeding, alongside the road."

Tink had gone pale, and I was standing there dumb as a fence post.

A slow smile worked its way across Johnson's face. "Why don't you two just go bring the sheriff around now?" He gave a chuckle, standing there seeing us struck with fear. He knew we weren't going for the sheriff.

We rode out of Devil's Falls hungover, sick in the stomach, and penniless. As we left the town limits behind us, Tink mumbled, "That was *not* a good town."

I was too down-at-the-mouth to say a word, but I fully agreed with him. They knew we'd done the robbery, and that eighteen thousand dollars was the price we had to pay to keep anyone from telling on us. It was a powerful lot of money, but considering a rope was waiting for us on some hangman's gallows, I was willing to take the loss.

It left us in a desperate situation. We were dead broke with no prospects for any immediate relief. We'd have to either find a job or go back to the only occupation either of us knew. And without Waldo there to help . . . I shook my head. We were in a bad way.

As soon as we were far enough away from Devil's Falls we turned north and hid out a couple days in the Superstition Mountains, nursing our headaches, washing our clothes in a stream, and shooting a couple long-legged jacks to fill our cookpot. We talked about our future, and bleak as it appeared to be, we couldn't stay holed up in the mountains forever. So, two days later, feeling and smelling better, Tink and I rode into a little town called Casa Grande and burgled a drugstore.

But we hadn't counted on there being a dog inside. I lost a patch out of my britches to its snapping teeth before we were finally clear of town and riding like the wind.

Hungry and depressed, we stuck up a freight wagon driven by an old man and a little boy. Waldo would have been proud of the daylight robbery, except that we rode away from there with only two dollars and some change. It was enough for a meal a few hours later at a place called Walton's Springs. Walton's Springs was a hole in the wall, like Devil's Falls, and there was enough in common between the two names that we didn't want to hang around long, or talk to anyone.

We rode out the daylight and come night found ourselves camped out on the desert pondering our dilemma. Over the following weeks and months we worked our way south again, always one step ahead of starvation and the law, leaving a string of angry shop owners and clerks in our wake. If we were only marginal desperadoes under Waldo's guidance, we were complete failures on our own. It must have been mulish determination that kept us trying again and again. That or sheer folly . . . and the idea that we could eventually succeed in this if only we gave ourselves enough time and managed to stay out of jail.

Winter was cold and wet and generally miserable. We finally took a job in the town of Stafford, working for a freight hauler named Gershwin, mucking out stalls in his livery for fifty cents a day, a meal, and room at the back of the stables with a potbelly stove and two cots. We didn't try robbing anybody that winter, not wanting to hold up shops where we were living. We weren't that dense!

The work was hard, but at least we slept well—warm and with a peace of mind that I'd not known for nearly two years. But life was hard. We celebrated the passing of the old year at the Episcopal church, where most the town had gathered to ring in 1902 with a toast of ginger punch. Tink and me, we'd pretty much sworn off liquor after our disaster in Devil's Falls. Afterward, alone in our six-by-ten room, we lamented our situation. A man can't hardly live on what we were earning, and time was passing us by. We were no better off in 1902 than we had been in 1899 when we'd left Bisbee—maybe even worse! With a renewed sense of determination, we decided to strike out again come spring.

And that's just what we did. We spent a month wandering aimlessly northward, making our way slowly toward the White Mountains, just because Tink and me had never seen them before. And that's how we come to be in Clifton one fine spring day, eyeing the Clifton Merchant's Bank with empty pockets and a gnawing hunger in our bellies. Desperation makes men do desperate things, and what Tink and I were contemplating was certainly that.

Tink adjusted his bandanna around his neck and checked the loads in his Colt revolver. I was still using the Forehand and Wadsworth, as we never seemed to get far enough ahead for me to replace the Colt I'd lost in our botched daylight robbery of that barbershop in Oro Blanco.

216

"I'll just stroll in there real casual-like and take a look," I told him. "You be waiting right here by the door."

A woman stepped out of the bank and two men entered.

"It's sorta busy," Tink noted worriedly. "What do you think Waldo would have done?"

I grimaced. "He'd have said the more people there was in there, the more pockets we could pick clean."

"Yeah, he would. I don't like this, Howie."

"I'm usually the one who says that."

Tink's blue eyes glinted in the sunlight as a small grin lifted his sunburned cheeks. "You must be rubbing off on me."

Our horses were ready. All we had to do was make our move. I went inside the bank and glanced around. There were two men by the clerk's windows and two more in line, and a woman holding a little boy's hand. I was wound up tighter than a spring as I stepped back outside. For the moment the sidewalk was empty.

"Now or never," I said in a low voice.

"Let's get it over with, Howie."

We drew our guns and reached for our masks, preparing to pull them over our noses as we made our move. Then we turned into the doorway.

Something was wrong. We hadn't said a

word, but the clerks and two of the men already had their hands stretched toward the ceiling. The woman was hugging the child. She looked terrified. And then we realized what was happening. I think there is a word for experiencing something that has already happened, but I couldn't think of it. I did remember the lonely store on the way to Tombstone, and how we'd busted in right in the middle of a holdup. And of all the rotten luck, it was happening to us again!

They weren't wearing masks, but they were carrying guns. One of them turned as we came through the door, and his eyes widened at the guns we were carrying. The next thing I knew, he was shooting at us. Then all hell broke loose and I dove to the floor. People scattered and wood splintered. An inkwell shattered. I threw a couple wild shots in the direction of the teller cages where the bank robbers were making their stand, hoping I wouldn't hit a clerk or innocent bystander, then rolled under a table. One of the desperadoes took a shot at me, and as his bullet zinged past my ear I took aim at his fleeing legs.

My ears filled with the roar of gunfire and the screams of the woman. A man grunted, another gave out a cry, and as suddenly as it began, the shooting stopped. I couldn't believe I was living through all this again. Cautiously I unfolded myself and crawled out.

Two men were down. Another leaned against the cages, buckled and gripping his side. A tall fellow whom I recognized as one of the patrons was standing nearby, a six-shooter in his fist, his quick eyes darting this way and that.

I stood, and the man said, "You two showed up just in time."

The woman huddling in a corner was unharmed. Another man poked his head out from around the teller cages. In a moment the tellers appeared too, and then men began streaming in from the street. Tink had been crouched in another corner, and he stood, wiping his sweaty face with his bandanna.

"Yeah," I replied, not knowing what else to say. I couldn't believe what I was hearing. Could the same thing happen twice? He thought we had tried to *stop* the robbery. I felt as if I was reliving a dream. But it hadn't been a dream. It had been real. Both times. I remembered how Waldo had twisted it around to make us look like heroes. I steeled myself and, giving Tink a glance, said, "We heard what was happening and figured we'd get the drop on those outlaws."

A heavyset man in a suit, wearing a big, gold belly chain and puffing as if he'd jogged from some considerable distance, came over and pumped our hands. "Thank you, sirs, thank you for saving my bank!" he declared.

Tink nodded, still wearing a confused look. I said he was welcome.

A sheriff came in next, surveyed the scene, then began asking a lot of questions, which we mostly answered in an honest way. Tink and me, we tried to leave, but they'd have none of that. Finally they hauled those three bank robbers out of there, and I learned that a fourth man ended up in custody after trying to hobble out of town with a bullet in his calf.

Things calmed down after that, and we were just about to leave when the banker came out of his back office and pushed twenty dollars gold into each of our hands and thanked us again for showing up when we did.

We took the money, feeling half proud of ourselves. But just like the last time, that good feeling was tinged by knowing that we had been there to do the same thing those other men had tried. We'd been twice lucky. That hardly ever happens to a man. I thought about that long and hard as Tink and I headed to a nearby restaurant.

Chapter Seventeen

"That was a close one," Tink said as he wolfed down a forkful of mashed potatoes covered in thick, brown gravy.

"This is almost too strange," I said.

"Yeah. Sorta gives you the shivers all over."

"You feel like someone is trying to tell us something?"

Tink looked up from his plate where his knife was working its way through the thick steak. "You talking about God?"

I shrugged. Tink never put much stock in religion. "Well, it is a strange coincidence, don't you think?"

"Ain't that what coincidences are, Howie? I mean, if they never happened, no one would have ever invented a word for them, right?"

"I hadn't thought about it that way." Now I had something else to ponder.

Tink looked past my shoulder. "Here comes that man," he said around a mouthful of well-done beef.

Footsteps sounded on the floor behind me. I turned to find the man from the bank, the one who'd helped out after the shooting had started. He grinned and stuck out a hand. "Afternoon, gentlemen," he said. His voice was deep, his face sunburned, his hands hard as leather. Although there was a smile on his face, I detected a sternness behind it as if this fellow took life too seriously, as if he had a mission and would pursue it with Apache-like doggedness. "Mind if I join you for a few minutes?"

Tink motioned toward a vacant chair, swallowed down his food, and said, "You're welcome to, if you want."

I was feeling nervous about this, but Tink seemed at ease, so maybe I was just worrying too much.

"My name is Burton Mossman," he said, and since he already knew ours, we just nodded and told him it was a pleasure to make his acquaintance.

"You two were pretty coolheaded back at the bank when all that shooting broke out," he said.

I almost laughed. I'd been scared to death!

"Yeah, well, me and Howie, we've have faced desperadoes before," Tink went on easily, reading his lines from a page out of Waldo's book. There was a mischievous glint in his eyes that I suppose only I noticed, for Mossman was nodding his head, looking impressed.

"I could tell that," he said, "and frankly, that's why I've come looking for you now."

"Oh?" I was suddenly curious.

"I'm looking for some good men. Thought maybe you two might just fit the bill."

"Good men for what reason, Mr. Mossman?" I asked.

He fished an envelope from an inside vest pocket and removed a sheet of paper, passing it over to me. It was a letter from Governor Nathan Oakes Murphy. I read it with interest, surprise showing on my face.

"What is it?" Tink asked when I finished.

I handed it across to him. "Governor Murphy is organizing the Arizona Rangers—again."

"That's right, and I'm to be the captain," Mossman said. "I've been scouting around for fourteen good men, and my privates and I still have room for a couple more. I'd like to offer you two the jobs."

I knew a little about the Arizona Rangers. They had existed twice before, once in 1860 and again in 1882. Both times the organization had been short-lived. The Civil War had disbanded them the first time. A lack of funding had done the same the second.

As if reading my thoughts, Mossman said, "The twenty-first Arizona Legislative Assembly has approved funding for the Rangers. I've been authorized to offer fifty-five dollars a month to the men I pick to come on board with us."

"Fifty-five a month?" Tink blurted, his eyes leaping up from the letter to stare at Mossman.

"That's the approved pay for a private."

For two fellows who'd been walking a tightrope over poverty gulch for so many years, fifty-five a month sounded like a royal sum of money. Made me feel like Mr. J. D. Rockefeller!

"What would we have to do?" I asked.

"You'd take on the full responsibilities of a lawman. Only, the whole territory would be your jurisdiction. Mostly you two would carry out your duties down here in this southern region. There's been an increase in rustlers, as you may well be aware. Driving them out of the mesquite breaks and into jail is our main concern. And there are plenty of other outlaws roaming through the territory that the Rangers would be required to hunt down and bring to justice too."

The offer was enticing. Tink looked excited

about it too. I told Mossman we'd have to talk it over and get back to him.

"Good. You two do that. I'm staying at the White Mountain Hotel until tomorrow, then I'm heading south to set up our headquarters. The Rangers are all planning to meet up there next month."

He shook our hands again, then folded that letter back into its envelope. "Hope to hear from you later today."

Through the window we watched Burton Mossman stroll toward a big, white hotel across the street. When he'd disappeared inside, Tink's view shifted back to me. "What do you think, Howie?"

"It's a real good opportunity."

"It's a great opportunity!" he said excitedly. "I think we ought to take the job."

I did too.

Becoming Arizona Rangers did two things for us. It gave us respectability as well as the perfect alibi for our other business. And it finally brought Tink and me back to Bisbee. Bisbee was where Mr. Mossman had decided to set up the Rangers' headquarters.

Two weeks after signing on with Burt Mossman, Tink and I rode into Bisbee, accompanied by three other newly minted Rangers. I was looking forward to seeing my family again, but apprehensive. What was I to tell them I'd been doing these last two years? Coming home a Ranger lent an air of respectability to Tink and me, but our past was something I could never reveal to them. It would devastate Ma and Pa. Yet I'd never been comfortable giving a lie. So instead of immediately riding up the hill to the little house where I'd spent so many years, I went with Tink down into Brewery Gulch to hash through what we were going to tell my family and his.

We finally decided to admit to some aimless wandering and taking on a few odd jobs now and then to carry us along. We were thinking mainly of our wintering-over in Stafford. And certainly robbing and burglarizing would be considered odd enough jobs. We just had to be careful about letting on too much about what sort of work we'd actually done.

That decided, we got ourselves settled in at company headquarters. Evening was coming on when we finally changed into clean shirts and pinned on our shiny new badges. I paused in front of a mirror on the way out, having a hard time moving on for some reason. Outside, we strolled to where our horses were tied. I was walking maybe a mite taller than usual, and grinning as we saddled up. Tink went to his folks' house while I rode across town to mine.

The old gate still had a squeak. The path to the front steps looked unchanged; weeds encroached on it, kept at bay only by constant foot travel. It was nearly dark when I climbed the steps to the front porch. A warm glow was coming from behind the drawn curtains. Feeling a strange apprehension, I rapped on the door.

There was the sound of footsteps beyond, interspersed with the regular tap of a walking stick on the floor. The handle turned, and there was Ma. Her eyes widened, and then her face broke out in a smile.

"Howard!"

"Ma."

"John," she called, turning back to the house. "Howard's come home!"

I gave her a hug. There was a commotion, and suddenly Anne and Beth's faces were poking past Ma. Excited, they both gave me a hug and pulled me into the house. They had grown so much, I hardly recognized them. Anne, though she was youngest, was fully as tall as Beth. And Ma, it seemed to me, had shrunk a good three or four inches. Then I recalled that I'd grown some too over the last two years.

Inside, Pa was sitting in his chair. He didn't get up when I came in. I was afraid he was still disappointed in my decision to leave with Tink and Waldo, but I was prepared to defend myself. Then I saw why he didn't rise.

"Pa! What happened?" I stepped over where the light was better.

"Howard," he said, and a grim smile came to his face. His face seemed a lot older, but I wasn't looking at it. It was his legs I was staring at. My voice cracked a bit, and I asked him again.

The smile tightened to a grimace. "Accident at the mine. About eight months ago. Cable snapped on one of the steam shovels. Bucket come down." He paused a moment, then made a sound like a knife slice. "Cut 'em off like a guillotine."

The room went silent, and I sensed the tension in the three women behind me. "I'm sorry, Pa," I said. I suddenly wished I'd been there to help out. I should have been.

The tight grin returned. "Things happen, Howard. The Lord gives each of us our own cross to bear. He's given me this one, and I'll be okay. It's not up to the clay to tell the potter how he is to shape up his vessels, now, is it?"

I gulped and shook my head. "I don't know, Pa."

"But you're home now, and safe. My prayers have been answered." The smile broadened, and then he spied the Rangers badge. "Say,

Howard, what's this?" Reaching out, he touched it. "Are you a lawman?"

Ma and the girls clamored around for a look. I had been so proud of it only a few minutes ago. But now, seeing Pa like this, it didn't matter so much.

"Arizona Ranger," I said softly, without any excitement.

"A Ranger!" Beth exclaimed. "But I learned in school that the Rangers disappeared twenty years ago."

"They did. Governor Murphy has just reorganized them. Burton Mossman is the new captain, and he's setting up headquarters right here in Bisbee." I told them how it had come about, how we'd stopped the bank robbery, and how Burt Mossman had been in that bank at the time. When I'd finished, Pa sat there shaking his head.

"The Lord works in mysterious ways."

"Yes, he does," Ma affirmed, putting an arm around my waist and drawing me closer. "And He's brought Howard back home to us."

"Where's Tink? And how about Waldo?" Anne asked, her eyes bright, her face beaming. I could hardly believe how she'd grown.

I spent the next hour giving them a carefully edited account of my life for the past two years. When I finished the girls were bubbling with questions, but Pa only sat there, his mouth cocked to one side as he pondered what I'd just told them. It made me uneasy, but I hadn't time to dwell on that. Ma wanted to feed me, and the girls wanted to know what towns I'd seen and what the women there were wearing. I hadn't noticed much of that, except briefly in Devil's Falls, where the abundance of pretty young women seemed strangely out of balance with the rest of the population.

Thinking about Devil's Falls still left a sour taste in my mouth, but if Tink and I hadn't lost everything there, we wouldn't be Arizona Rangers now. The way things had worked out sort of lessened the sting of that experience.

I spent the night in the parlor on the old sofa. I slept well, and the next morning had breakfast with the family. Ma wheeled Pa in from the bedroom, and he led the family in prayer. Nothing much had changed over the two years I'd been gone, I decided, except that now Pa was a cripple and the family depended on the money Ma earned from Mr. Deavers. It seemed unfair that she should have to work so hard. But I knew if I said so, both Ma and Pa would simply say that life is not necessarily fair. They were the sort of people who accepted their lot with quiet resignation.

I wasn't so inclined.

I left for Rangers headquarters the next morning, promising to be back for dinner that night. Anne ordered me to tell Tink hello from her as Ma reached up and tried to tame my cowlick. I shied from her fussing there on the front porch, went to where I'd left my horse, and rode down into town.

Chapter Eighteen

After that, little more was ever asked about what Tink and I had been up to while we were gone. The subject of Waldo would come up from time to time, and in private Tink and I would speculate on our ex-partner. We both figured he'd drifted on, landed in some jail, maybe even seen the hangman. Waldo was certainly headed in that direction.

We had taken rooms in a boardinghouse, having outgrown our families' homes. Every month I sent part of my paycheck over to help Ma and Pa. Pa had a little money coming in from the miners' union, but Ma still had to work the laundry. Prices kept going up faster than her pay.

There was still a matter of about seventy dollars that I felt responsible for. Over the next year I managed to save it up, and one afternoon, when I was visiting Ma, Mr. Deavers had stepped outside and I slipped around the counter and put the money at the back of the drawer.

I felt better after that. I knew there were a lot of other folks who deserved to be paid back too, but like Pa would say, "You do what you can in this world." And that's what I was doing.

Tink and I sometimes recalled the old days, and we'd joke about joining the Rangers only because we had thought it would be the perfect alibi for our *other* job. But the truth of it is, neither one of us had enjoyed robbing folks very much. That life was all behind us. Now we were helping folks, and that felt a whole lot better.

Beth married a miner named Robert Witchell in the spring of 1903. Witchell was a solid, down-to-earth fellow, a shift boss at the Copper Queen mine and a deacon at our church.

I wheeled Pa up the aisle so that he could give her away. He was dressed in his suit, a collar, and a tie. His graying hair was slicked down so that it gleamed in the morning sunlight. Ma was pretty in a plain gray dress. She smiled serenely through the ceremony, now and then touching her eyes with the handkerchief she clutched. But Ma was looking old and tired.

Anne, at fifteen, had shaped up to be the prettiest gal in all of Bisbee. And that fact hadn't gone unnoticed by the local population of young men. But Anne showed no interest in any of them. She had eyes only for Tink. She had always had eyes for Tink, and now, blossoming and gaining in poise and confidence, she was making her move. She'd asked Tink to sit with her after the ceremony, when the guests had packed into the tiny basement room of the church for punch and cakes.

I wasn't too surprised when Tink agreed. And there had been no jokes about pulling her pigtails, this time. The pigtails had gone the way of rag dolls and make-believe tea parties. Anne's hair was long, shining copper, held in place with a simple blue ribbon. The other young men there could only drool with envy while Tink, looking handsome in his suit and neatly trimmed beard, merely grinned.

I was promoted to sergeant that year, and we chased rustlers in and out of the mesquite breaks and dragged them up out of Mexico, where they had run off to hide. Train robbers were big business for us too, and we rounded up a couple of bank robbers as well.

It was late in October when word reached Rangers headquarters that a train had been stopped outside of Tucson and a car carrying gold had been blown up. The gang that did it had killed two guards and taken money and jewelry from the passengers. One of the desperadoes had badly pistol-whipped a man, leaving him nearly dead. According to the witnesses, the men fled southeast. Another report had these same villains moving toward the Dragoon Mountains, and the governor requested Ranger assistance in rounding them up.

Five of us—me, Pete Whal, J. E. Campbell, Dave Allison, and Harry Wheeler, along with a half-breed tracker named Ben "Lizard Tail" Hennigan—headed out the next morning. Tink wasn't with us, as a few days earlier Captain Rynning—Burt Mossman had resigned in 1902—had sent him over to San Rafael to take charge of some rustlers who had been caught with a red-hot running iron and four cows tied to a tree.

After talking to the witnesses and scouting around for a trail, Ben spied their trace and we were onto them. Ben was old enough to have known Geronimo personally, although he always denied it. Sunburned and black-haired, he could almost pass for an Indian, and I think the ties to his Apache relatives were closer than he wanted to let on. He knew his business when it came to tracking, and inside of two days we'd worked our way deep into the Dragoons, where long ago Cochise had lived and hidden out. It was rough country and a good place to flee to if you wanted to escape the U.S. Cavalry—or an outfit of Arizona Rangers.

We'd wound our way down into a little, dry valley, nestled between two jagged peaks. It was oven-hot in spite of the lateness of the year. Hunkered down over a bare rock, Ben frowned. He ran a finger along a bright gouge in the rock, then looked up and squinted ahead. "They passed by here. Not long ago."

"Which way?" Pete Whal asked.

Ben lifted a finger and pointed.

"Let's go get them," I said. We'd been on their trail long enough, and I wanted to get this over with.

Ben's dark eyes came around. "They could be setting us up for an ambush, Sergeant Blake."

"How can they know we're trailing 'em?" Campbell asked.

"I would know," Ben said flatly.

"Yeah, but you're you," I replied. "A ghost couldn't sneak up on you, Ben."

He grinned tightly as he swung back onto his horse. "Just keep both your eyes wide open, Sarg." He struck out in the lead. The valley funneled into a rocky ravine where the crack of the horses' iron shoes made me nervous. Finally Ben brought us to a halt and motioned for us to dismount. Leaving our animals, we pressed on afoot. Here and there were signs of the passage of horses that even I could read. Ben paused over a snapped twig, tasted the exposed end, and frowned. We wondered what exactly that meant, but Ben moved on without saying a word.

Then all at once I smelled smoke.

Ben raised a hand for us to stop, then signaled to split and advance. Allison and I skirted around to the right while Ben and the others pressed to the left. We worked our way over some boulders until we spied them about two hundred feet off, their gear spread out like they intended to spend the night. The four men were hunched over a small campfire with three of them showing us their backs. The fourth one, the one facing me, took off his hat and mopped his bald head with a red bandanna. There was something familiar about that one. I squinted against the harsh light but couldn't place where I'd seen him before.

Across the way Ben and the others were in place. We drew our guns. Now that he'd found them, Ben's job was through. He'd back us up if we needed it, but for now it was the Rangers' job to round up these desperadoes. I gave a nod to the others and we crept down toward those men, keeping low until the very last moment.

Then we had them flanked. It had been our experience that when you find your quarry and catch them with their hands empty, they nearly always reach for the clouds and come in peacefully.

"Arizona Rangers!" I shouted. "Hands in the air!"

Well, *nearly* always.

One of them dove out of the line of fire and drew his gun. Its boom filled the air, and across the way Pete Whal gave a startled cry as the bullet spun him around.

There was no time to think. The men down below scattered like startled quail, and we were all firing at each other as we dove for cover. I targeted the man who had shot Pete and fired. My bullet ricocheted off a rock and he scooted away, running a zigzag back down a ravine.

Gunfire was coming from all directions as I crawled out from behind a boulder in time to get a glimpse of the man fleeing around a clump of mesquite. Then he was gone.

I snapped a shot at one of the bandits taking refuge behind a rock by the fire pit. Leaping to my feet, I took off like a jackrabbit after the man who had fled down the ravine. The sound of gunfire faded behind me, while up ahead I caught glimpses of the man darting among the boulders. He spun around, and I flattened against the shoulder of sandstone as his bullet sprayed rock dust into my cheek.

I wheeled back and pinned him into a cleft of rock with two shots. He answered my challenge and then we were on the move again. I was gaining on him, mainly because he'd climbed into some pretty rough terrain. He found himself facing a sheer cliff with the only way out straight up. He grappled for a handhold, and I had a clear shot at him. I took it, but my bullet only chipped a piece of rock by his gun hand. With a yelp he dropped the revolver and grabbed his fingers. The gun clattered down a slope and stopped four or five feet below him.

"Hold up there if you want to keep breathing," I gasped, having trouble with that breathing part myself. He was winded too. I could see his back heaving as he clung there on the rock wall that had proved his undoing.

For an instant he didn't move, then all at once he laughed.

"Howie? Is that you, old partner?"

"Waldo?" I slung the sweat from my eyes as he let himself down off the rock and turned to face me. Waldo Fritz hadn't changed much. He was a little older, a little heavier, and a lot more dangerous. His dark eyes shifted toward where the gun lay nearby, then back at me.

"Well, well, well. Look at you, Howie. An Arizona Ranger? Who'd have ever guessed?"

"I figured you'd left the Territory years ago. Either that or you'd met up with a hangman somewhere."

"Me? No, I'm too smart for that."

"You're not looking very smart now."

He shrugged, and shifted a few steps to his right. "How have you been, old partner?"

"Doing all right." I stepped around so that I could keep an eye on him. Those dark eyes followed me, narrowing slightly. Suddenly a tight smile lifted his sharp cheeks.

"And Tink?"

"He's a Ranger too. And if you're thinking of going for that gun, don't." I motioned for him to step back, but he didn't move.

"I don't think you are going to stop me, Howie. Not with an empty gun."

Empty? I hadn't kept count of my shots, but then, he might have been bluffing too. Waldo was a master at bluffing his way out of trouble.

"I think I have a bullet left," I said, trying to sound confident.

"Do you?" Now the smile widened. "I can see from here that the cylinders are empty." He moved toward the gun on the ground.

I pulled the trigger, and the hammer snapped down on a spent cartridge. He dove for the gun. Instinctively I stabbed for my pocket and re-

A Good Town

trieved the little derringer that I'd been carrying
ever since I'd taken it from that dead man's fingers all those years ago. I leaned forward, its
muzzle pointed at Waldo's head. He stopped,
eyes wide, showing fear for the first time.

"This one is loaded," I said evenly.

He backed off.

I grabbed up the Colt revolver and tucked it
under my belt. "Let's get back with the others."

"Can't we talk about this, Howie?" he said,
regaining that easy confidence.

"Nothing to talk about, Waldo. I'm taking you
in."

"You don't have to do it, Howie. You could
just let me go—for old times' sake?"

"I can't do that, Waldo."

"What about the time when that barber got
the drop on you and I saved you? You owe it to
me."

"Already paid you back for that by busting
you out of jail, remember?"

"Oh, yeah." He lowered himself to the
ground, where there was some shade.

I took a nearby rock that was out of the sun
too.

"Doesn't friendship mean anything?"

"Sure it does, Waldo. But this badge means
something too."

He smiled and nodded. "It's important to you,

241

ain't it? A job you can feel proud doing?"

"Something like that. I kept my eyes open. Haven't ever seen or heard anything of the Fritz Gang. I figured you left the Territory."

"The Fritz Gang." He gave a short laugh. "I haven't thought about that for years." A reflective tone softened his voice. "I grew up some, Howie. I figured if I wanted to be successful at this profession, then I'd have to keep my name out of the papers."

"Boy, that's a change."

"Yeah. Guess we all change." He laughed. "Well, look at you, Howie. Who could guess that four or five years ago you were holding up drugstores and mine payrolls." He gave a look that made me suddenly uneasy. "I was really sore about you and Tink walking out on me like you did."

"You were taking us where we didn't want to go, Waldo. We had to leave."

"I suppose not everyone is cut out for this kind of life." He paused, thoughtfully chewing his lip. "Let me go, Howie. No one ever needs to know what happened here."

"I already told you I can't."

"Can't or won't?"

"Is there a difference?"

"Reckon there ain't." He studied the badge on my vest. "You understand if you take me in, I'm going to have to tell about us—you and me and Tink. How we spent all those years robbing and burglarizing. How you two were part of that payroll heist where those two men died?" His dark eyebrows arched speculatively, and there was a threatening glint in those cool, contemplating eyes. "That would be a shame, wouldn't it, Howie, if folks were to learn how you lived your life before going straight? The Rangers would take that shiny badge away from you and throw you in jail, wouldn't they?"

A knot twisted my gut as he sat there considering me. He'd been holding that trump card all along, and he knew it. He twisted the knife a little deeper.

"Did you ever tell your family about it?" he asked, as if it were an afterthought.

"No."

"If I remember right, you said your pa's a religious man. How do you think he would take to the news?"

I hated myself right then. Hated myself for all the stupid things I'd ever done. A shiver gripped my chest as hopelessness squeezed the breath from it. "You'd leave the Territory?"

"Sure I would."

"And not come back?"

"Believe me, Howie, this part of the country has become way too hot for me to stick around.

243

You turn your back and I'm outta here. You'll never see nor hear a peep out of Waldo Fritz again."

He glanced at the tiny gun in my hand. "I'm surprised you kept that," he said.

"It reminds me of where I've been, so that I don't ever go back there again." I lowered the hammer and shoved it into my pocket. "Get out of here, Waldo. Get out and keep moving and don't ever come back."

He stood and offered his hand.

I just looked at it.

"I don't blame you. How about my gun?"

"No. No gun."

He gave a tight grin, nodded, and turned back to the rock face. In a moment he'd scrambled up over it and was gone. I stood there as if I had become part of the gray landscape. I knew I hadn't done the right thing, yet what else could I have done? Slowly I became aware that the shooting had ceased and that there was the sound of footsteps coming up behind me.

"There you are, Howard," Campbell said, looking suddenly relieved. "I saw you take after that one. I was afraid he'd got the jump on you."

"Got away," I said, looking at the straight, gray rock.

"Well, can't get them all. But we have the ones he left behind. He drop that?"

I glanced at Waldo's revolver. "Yeah. Dropped it going up over that cliff. I lost one just like it a few years back. I think I'll just hold on to this one. How is Whal?"

"Took one in the leg. Wheeler is doctoring him now."

When we left that ravine I felt I was leaving something behind. Something important.

We'd had one wounded. They had two, a third man dead, and one escaped. At least that's how the report would read. I hunkered down over the dead man. His head was bald as a rock, and there was a scar slashed down across one eyebrow—and then I remembered. This was the same man I'd freed from that Tombstone jail when we'd sprung Waldo. Somehow they'd gotten together after we'd split up. I shook my head, wondering how much suffering I'd let loose because of that . . . wondering how much I'd let loose just now.

Frowning, I stood and helped load him onto his horse. And then we hauled the desperadoes out of those harsh mountains and back to Bisbee.

Chapter Nineteen

There were a few young ladies about Bisbee who caught my eye, but so far none had star-struck me so much that I wanted to hitch my wagon to hers. I wasn't ready for that sort of settling down yet. Something was holding me back from getting too involved, an image that I carried around in my brain of the sort of woman I really wanted—a very fuzzy image, but real nonetheless. Besides, my Ranger job kept me on the move, and that wouldn't have been fair to a new bride.

Over the years Tink and I had had a chance to scout out a lot of potentially good towns. So far we hadn't found anything that was much better than Bisbee, and besides, right then Tink wasn't all that keen on the idea of moving anyway. He and Anne were seeing each other on a regular basis, and Tink had taken to eating meals at my folks' home more often than I did. He even started attending services on Sunday mornings!

The year came and went and I was still helping Ma with the family finances. Pa had his stipend from the miners' union, but he had also begun to write articles for the *Union Journal*, which was published four times a year. The miners' union had even bought him a second-hand Remington typewriter, which he set up on a table in the parlor next to his chair. The newspapers sometimes asked Pa to write a column for them too, and that brought in a few extra dollars a month.

In May of 1905, Beth had a little boy and named him John Robert. He had the smallest hands and the brightest blue eyes I'd ever seen, and when I held him against my chest the tiny bundle seemed to disappear into my arms. I noted how Tink and Anne kept exchanging glances the first time they saw little Johnny. At sixteen years old, Anne was beautiful and all grown up, and I figured she was developing notions of starting a family of her own.

Tink had settled down over the last couple of years. He hardly ever talked about finding that "good town" anymore. I was a little disappointed, because I was itching to move on again and see the world. I reckon the bitterness of the last time we'd tried that was far enough behind me now that I was forgetting what it had tasted like.

I rarely ever thought of our mishap at Devil's Falls anymore. That part of my life and everything connected with it had faded into the foggy past. And good riddance. Life was shaping up all right for Tink and me. I was still a sergeant in the Rangers, but I felt sure that I had a good shot at making captain someday, if Wheeler ever quit. Harry Wheeler had replaced Tom Rynning as captain in 1904. Wheeler had been chosen over me, I was told, because he was older. The Rangers were now up to twenty-six men, and there were rumblings coming out of the governor's office that funding was getting tight.

It was in May of 1906, exactly one year after John Robert was born, that Tink, his hat crushed in his fingers, went to Pa to ask for Anne's hand in holy matrimony. "Holy matrimony." Those were the very words Tink used. Anne had just turned seventeen and was prettier than a valley filled with rainbow cactuses in June. Tink was nearly twenty-four, and he had a good, steady job. That was important to Pa.

Pa considered the request and told Tink he'd

give him an answer the following Sunday. Tink was a nervous wreck all week, but after we'd wheeled Pa out of church on the appointed morning and Pa gave him his blessings, Tink let out a whoop and flung his hat high into the air.

The date was set, and Anne and Ma and Beth threw themselves into planning the event. Meanwhile, Tink bungled his way through his days at work like a three-legged mule. Captain Wheeler was about to ship him off to California until he could get his head down out of the clouds, but before he did, the telegram came through.

Wheeler figured it was a gift from heaven. I thought so too at the time. We'd been having an unusually quiet spell in our corner of the Territory, nary a rustler or a bank robber to break the monotony of the days.

"Here's something to keep your mind busy," Wheeler said, staring pointedly at Tink. We'd been summoned into his office and were standing before the cluttered oak desk.

"What is it?" I asked.

"This just came in from Elfrida. Seems there's some problem there. A missing man." He handed the telegram to me. "As you can see, it's rather vague, but the town sheriff is requesting Ranger assistance. And he has asked for you two by name." Wheeler narrowed his eyes suspiciously. "Who do you two know in Elfrida?"

I didn't recognize the name on the telegram and passed it over to Tink. Tink only shrugged at my puzzled look, flashing one of his crooked grins. Tink hadn't been thinking clearly for weeks, and I don't know why I should have expected him to start now.

"I don't know," I said, doing a brief search of my memory and coming up blank.

"Well, anyway, it will be good for you two to get out of town for a while—especially you, dreamy-eyes." Wheeler snatched the paper from Tink's hands.

Tink left word with Anne that we'd be gone a few days. We packed our saddlebags, tied up our bedrolls, stopped on our way out of town for provisions, and then headed north toward Tombstone.

We'd been on the road for less than an hour when all at once I blurted, "Marshal Berger?"

That snapped Tink out of his reverie. "Of course. Who else could it be?"

But there was a problem. I narrowed my gaze at him. "That was"—I tallied up the years—"six years ago, wasn't it?"

"Sounds about right."

"We weren't Rangers then, Tink. How would Berger know to ask for us by name?"

"Hmmm. Maybe he read about all our daring

exploits in the newspapers, eh, Howie?" Tink puffed out his chest and struck a pose.

I frowned. "Don't think so."

"Oh." He deflated before my eyes. "Well, maybe he just got hold of a roster from someplace? The governor?"

"That's more likely. Even so, what in the world would ever make him remember us? I mean, we were only two days out of his life. Heck, I had to search my brain for hours to come up with his name."

"What does that say about your brain, Howie?"

I shot him a glance. "Look who's talking, *dreamy-eyes*."

Tink laughed good-naturedly.

I rummaged around among those old memories. "Hey, wonder how little Alice is getting along."

"She was a cute kid."

"Yeah," I said, smiling, remembering that week we'd spent together; how she clung to me as I pulled her up out of that open mine shaft; how she had curled up in my arms afterward and cried.

"Wonder if she's still there," Tink mused.

"Why wouldn't she be?"

He rolled his eyes. "Figure it out, Howie. She'd be seventeen. The same age as Anne. She could be married and gone by now."

"Married and gone?" I hadn't even considered that. I tried to picture Alice a grown-up woman, and all I could come up with was the little girl we'd rescued from those desperadoes all those years ago. Tink's suggestion weighed heavy on me for the rest of the afternoon. I didn't understand why it should. I was hoping he was wrong. I really wanted to see little Alice again.

We arrived in Elfrida the next morning.

"This place hasn't changed much," Tink said as we rode into town from the west.

It hadn't—except that there were telephone lines strung on poles now. They ran along the main street and down the side streets. And electricity had come to town too. But what caught my eye were the horseless carriages parked on the road. Three of them. I wondered at the prosperity of the folks here in Elfrida. Not many people could afford to own one yet. But I had to smile when I noted that the machines had been stopped by the old hitching rails and tied there with ropes, as if they would up and wander away of their own accord if not tethered! I'll admit I knew next to nothing about these new contraptions, but I suspected that once the internal combustion engine had been shut down, they'd not drift off like a horse might.

"A good town for bandits, drunks, and cutthroats," I said, recalling Waldo's description of Elfrida all those many years before.

"A good town to die in," Tink quipped.

"Let's hope not."

We headed for the sheriff's office. It was right where we remembered it from our last visit, but now the weedy fields were gone. A building called a "garage" with a Standard Oil Company pump out front stood to the left of it. A bakery, spilling the delicious aroma of baking bread, crowded in to the right.

We turned our horses into the hitching rail and went inside. The office hadn't changed much either, except for the addition of another desk, which only crowded the floor more. A man was hunched over a desk, riffling through some papers. The face that glanced up at us when we entered was one I didn't recognize.

"Is Matt Tingley still around?" I asked.

He pushed his spectacles up the bridge of his nose and peered at us a moment. "Matt Tingley isn't here anymore," he replied. I caught the cautious tone in his voice. "You friends of his?"

"Met him once." I thumbed back the lapel of my vest and flashed the Rangers badge at him. His eyes widened owlishly behind the lenses.

"Ah, you've come." His face brightened. The sheriff was a thin fellow with a shock of unruly brown hair and brown eyes. When he stood to shake our hands he topped Tink and me by a good four inches, and I was only a whisker shy of six feet myself. His long hand was bony beneath my grip, but the shake was firm and sincere. "I'm Louis Crumm. I've been sheriff here for . . . ah . . . well, I have to tell you, Matt was killed about three years ago. I've been holding down the fort here ever since."

"Sorry to hear."

His wide mouth cocked down in a lopsided frown. "Yeah. It happens in our line of work, doesn't it?"

We understood that well enough. Over the years Tink and I had lost several Ranger friends in the course of performing their sworn duties. "Is Marshal Berger still around?" I asked.

"Berger? Don't you know?

"Know what?" Tink asked.

"Ed Berger is the reason I sent for you boys."

"The telegram only mentioned something about a missing person," I said.

Crumm frowned. "Ed turned up missing a couple weeks ago. We did what we could, but no one has been able to get a lead on what happened. That's when one of the local businessmen suggested we call in the Rangers. We agreed that would be the smartest thing to do, so that's when we sent for you two."

"You asked for us by name," Tink said wonderingly.

"That's right. He said you two were the best."

"He?" I inquired.

"Mr. Fritz. Owner of the Crystal Slipper Saloon. I got the feeling he knew you two."

"Fritz?" Tink croaked. We looked at each other.

"Waldo Fritz?" we both asked at the same time.

Crumm grinned. "Yep. That's the man. Him and Marshal Berger, they were pretty close. Fact is, Mr. Fritz is the only one aside from the marshal who saw the letter. Mr. Fritz is taking the marshal's disappearance in a real personal way."

That caught me off guard. Waldo Fritz, here in Elfrida? And a friend of Ed Berger? The last time I'd seen Waldo I'd told him to leave the Territory. Obviously, he hadn't.

"I . . . I guess I don't understand," I said, trying to gather my thoughts. "Waldo and Ed, they're friends?"

Crumm gave another one of his lopsided expressions, only this time it had reversed itself into a grin. "Well, sure they are. You might say they're almost family."

"Family?" Tink smirked.

Douglas Hirt

"Sure am. Mr. Fritz, he's about to marry that pretty little daughter of Ed's."

"Alice!" I yelped.

"Yep," he replied.

Tink and I stared at each other, then dove for the doorway.

We drew rein in front of the Silver Slipper Saloon and tied our mounts to the hitching rail, next to a shiny, maroon horseless carriage. A scrolled plaque right on the front of the machine spelled out the word "Cadillac," which we took to be the name of this particular horseless carriage. It was a handsome machine with black fenders and red pinstriping and four shiny brass lanterns. A large brass horn curled its way back to a big, black rubber bulb near the round steering tiller. Tink and I looked it over in mild amazement, never having seen so fancy a contraption before, then we put our minds back on business and stepped into the saloon.

It was a long, narrow affair, mostly unchanged from the last time we'd been here. Somehow the saloon looked smaller from the inside than it did from the outside. There were some men at tables, and a few others with their boots propped on the rail and their elbows leaning on the bar.

"What's your poison, fellas?" a beefy, jovial,

red-faced man with a huge purple nose asked. We stepped up to the shiny walnut plank and told the barkeeper we were looking for Waldo.

"Mr. Fritz is not taking visitors right now," he said, polishing a glass with a towel. "Now, what'll it be?"

Tink and I thumbed back our vests at the same time. The man's tiny eyes opened and the towel he'd been using on the glass stopped moving. "Arizona Rangers?"

"We need to see Waldo."

He cleared his throat. "I'll get him."

Chapter Twenty

The barkeeper shuffled from behind the polished plank and rapped quickly on a door. We were right there on his heels.

"Go away," growled a familiar voice from the other side.

"It's me, boss. There are a couple gents out here wanting to talk to you."

"Not now."

"Er, they're the Rangers you sent for, boss."

A long moment of silence passed. I thought I heard a high, muffled squeal and a giggle from beyond the door, then a harsh, urgent whisper. A piece of furniture scraped the floor, followed by the hurried taps of footsteps. It seemed to be taking Waldo an awful long time to reach the door. Finally it opened.

A Good Town

Waldo was a little older than I remembered, but in every other respect the same as that day I allowed him his freedom back in the Dragoon Mountains.

"Howie! Tink!" The sharp angles of his face shot up into a beaming smile as if we were his long-lost brothers. He pumped our hands enthusiastically and ushered us into the room, which looked to be a combination of an office and a sitting parlor. There was a long settee against one wall and a bookcase against another. Two stuffed chairs faced a table where an opened tantalus sat. Waldo's desk stood to one side near a safe and a two-drawer filing cabinet. The fresh fragrance of lilac hung heavily in the air, even though the season for lilacs was long past. The odor mixed curiously with the sharp tinge of whiskey and that long-forgotten but at once familiar smell of those cocaine cigarettes.

Waldo shot the bartender a quick, narrow glance before pulling the door shut in his face. When he turned back toward us, he was grinning again. "Drinks?" he offered, taking a decanter from the tantalus.

"No, thanks," I said. Tink just wagged his head.

Waldo set the decanter down. "Long time no see, partners." He waved us to the chairs and

259

flopped down on the settee, stretching out his long legs. As we took the seats my view shifted around the office and found a second door in the back wall, near a coat rack where a black frock and a holster and six-gun hung. Considering Waldo closer now, I detected a faint pink smudge on his white shirt. His hair was tousled and there seemed to be a rash developing on his neck.

"You've done all right for yourself, Waldo," Tink said, his gaze traveling around the room. "Still holding up two-bit stores on lonely stretches of highways?"

Waldo grinned, but there was no mirth in it. "No, no, Tink. No more of that for me. I had a life-changing experience." Waldo cocked a dark eye at me. "Howie here, he gave me a new lease on life. He ever tell you about that?"

"I did," I said, irritated with him for bringing it up.

"And that made me realize how badly I was squandering it. How precious life is," he mused, shaking his head. "The way I was going, I wouldn't have had many more years. No, I've gone straight, Tink," he said with a slick smile. "Bought me a respectable business and got me a girl."

A twinge stabbed me right between the ribs. I realized I was squeezing the arms of the chair and forced myself to release and to relax. "I let you go on the condition that you pack up and leave the Territory."

"You let me go to save your own neck, Howie," he came back dangerously. Then he smiled as if it was only a joke. "But if it makes you feel better, I did leave . . . for a while. Then one day down in a saloon in Fronteras I started to think, and I remembered this place. Something about it just drew me back here. And my timing couldn't have been better. The owner wanted to sell, and I happened to have a little cash."

"Stolen cash," Tink observed.

Waldo smiled thinly and shrugged his shoulders. "Not necessarily."

"We just came from talking with Sheriff Crumm," I broke in. "He said Ed Berger is missing. He said you two were friends . . . and something about a letter? What do you know about it?"

Waldo frowned and slowly shook his head. "Not a lot, I'm afraid, old friend. That's why we thought the Rangers could help. I can tell you what little I do know, although by now it's common knowledge throughout town. You ever hear of a man named Hastings Alvardo?"

The name had a familiar ring, but as far as I

knew the Rangers had never had any dealings with him.

Tink sat there with pursed lips and compressed eyes. "I think I might have seen a poster about the man at one time."

"You might very well have," Waldo went on. "Hastings and his brothers, Worton and Ernie, they held up a train about four years ago. It was carrying a military paymaster and a payroll bound for Fort Hauchuca. Since it was federal property he stole, that put it under Berger's jurisdiction."

Waldo paused as if to let us digest that. "Yes," I said impatiently, anxious for him to get on with his story.

Waldo grinned, folded his hands behind his head, and stared up at the ceiling. "Berger organized a posse and trailed the men back into the Chirichuas." He grinned, then glanced at us. "Funny how thieves and robbers always seem to flee to the mountains, eh?" He winked and shifted his view back to the tin tiles overhead. "To make a long story short, Berger caught up with Hastings and his brothers at a place called Blocks Canyon. There was gunplay, and Ernie was killed. Hastings and Worton, they took a couple slugs too, but lived to show the scars to their fellow inmates at Leavenworth Prison. At the trial, Hastings swore he'd come back for Ed and make him pay for killing Ernie."

"So somehow they managed to break out of Leavenworth Prison," I said, seeing where Waldo was heading with this.

"About six months ago."

"And Marshal Berger?" Tink pressed.

"He was advised of the breakout, of course, but he didn't seem too concerned. I reckon he wasn't taking Hastings's threat seriously."

"Most of the time they're only empty threats," I said. "When someone breaks out of a place like Leavenworth Prison, they don't usually hang around the States—or the Territories—waiting to be caught again. Usually they head south. Chile, Peru, Bolivia."

"Maybe." Waldo's voice hardened ever so slightly. "But for some men, revenge is everything." That dangerous look had suddenly returned.

"So, what happened?" I asked.

"He got a letter a couple weeks ago."

"From Hastings?" Tink asked.

"No . . . at least it didn't say so. There was no name signed to it. Ed showed it to me. The writer claimed he knew where Hastings and Worton were hiding out, and for fifty dollars, he'd tell Ed. He gave instructions about meeting him at some abandoned mining operations east of here."

Douglas Hirt

"And the marshal went? Alone?" I didn't even try to keep the incredulous tone from my voice.

Waldo nodded at the ceiling. "I told him I'd go with him. Even offered to drive him there in my automobile. But he said no. Said he'd go meet this man by himself."

I frowned. "You'd think a lawman with Marshal Berger's experience would know better than to go off like that by himself."

Waldo shrugged. "It wasn't the smartest thing that Ed Berger has ever done."

"Where is this letter now?" I asked.

"I don't know. It's disappeared. My guess is the marshal had it on him when he went to meet this man."

"And he never came back," Tink concluded.

"You got that right, bucko."

There was a knock on the door. Waldo scowled at the ceiling. "What is it now, Sam?" he called.

"Miss Haynes is here to see you, boss," came the reply from the other side.

Waldo swung his legs around and stood. "If there is nothing else, I've got a lady to see."

We stood too. The interview, at least for the moment, was over.

The barroom seemed busier than it had when we'd come in. I glanced around for Alice, not certain what she'd look like after all these years.

264

My brain still held the outdated picture of an eleven-year-old girl.

But there was no young woman in the saloon, and somehow I was relieved that she wasn't here. Waldo was heading toward the door, and we started after him. Suddenly the fragrance of lilacs was in the air again. Scanning the room as I moved, I spied the source of the odor standing at the bar, holding a shot glass in her fingers. She was an older, thickset woman, maybe thirty, with puffy, mascara-covered eyes and rouged cheeks. Her red beaded dress was cut low on top and stopped at about midcalf, brazenly exposing her limbs.

She looked us over with brazen temptation in her shadowed eyes as we made for the door. It was the same sort of look I recalled getting back in Devil's Falls. I'd grown up enough since then to understand the meaning of such an open invitation. I understood what this painted woman was all about—and all those other attractive ladies back in Devil's Falls, too. I remembered how the bartender, Hector Johnson, had given us a sly-fox grin when he'd told us that Phillip Swan ran a sort of "service business." We'd been pretty green back in those days.

Crumm had said that Waldo and Alice were engaged to be married. It suddenly angered me that Waldo and this woman had been together in his office—that he would do that to Alice.

Alice Haynes glanced up as we came to a stop there on the sidewalk. I need not have worried about recognizing her. I'd know that face anywhere. It was all grown up now, but the eyes, the small nose, the quick smile that came to her lips when she saw me, that was the Alice I remembered. She'd lengthened some, and filled out a lot—in all the right places. She was—she was—she was beautiful! I couldn't think of any other way to describe her. Put Alice Haynes and my sister, Anne, side by side and they'd be called the heartbreak twins, steamrolling their way through men's hearts.

Alice had been wearing a concerned look an instant before, but her eyes brightened upon seeing us. "Howie! And Tink!"

"Alice!" I fought down the urge to swing my arms around her and give her a big hug, and I had the feeling Tink did too. Then Waldo conveniently placed himself where a hug would have been impractical.

"You're all grown up," Tink exclaimed.

She smiled. Alice did indeed look all grown up in a white cotton dress with tiny pale blue flowers all over it. A wide straw bonnet kept the sun off her face, but her arms, bare below the puffed shoulders and quarter-length sleeves, were nut brown. Sun-darkened skin was definitely not fashionable with the women of 1906, but on Alice it looked wonderful.

Her view glanced off of Tink and lingered long and hard on me. I'd caught my breath. My heart was racing. We peered at each other like that a long moment before she turned back to Waldo.

"Have you heard anything?" Concern reshaped her face.

"Nothing yet, dear."

"Sheriff Crumm just told me you had finally arrived," she said, wheeling back to me. "Did Waldo tell you?"

"About Ed?" I grimaced. "He told us."

"You've got to help," she implored. "Waldo said you could. He said that if anybody could find him, the Arizona Rangers could."

"We'll do what we can, Alice," I said, wondering what Tink and I could accomplish that Crumm and the citizens of Elfrida couldn't.

Alice, Tink, and I went to see Gladys Berger. Gladys had aged since we'd last seen her. Her once brunette hair was now completely gray, and there seemed to be a bit more flesh about her green eyes, but all in all, the years had treated her kindly.

Upon our arrival Gladys told us how nice it was to see us again, and how handsome we'd both become, and that she prayed we could find her Ed for her, at which point her eyes began to brim and she apologized, turning away and patting them dry with a handkerchief. Alice put an arm around the older woman and gave her a hug.

The house had not changed in the least. Tink and I took the same, hard straight-back chairs we'd used all those years before while Alice and Gladys sat in the same settee. We spent a few minutes catching up and exchanging pleasantries before beginning our investigation.

"Did Ed say anything to you about this meeting he was suppose to have, Mrs. Berger?" I asked her.

"No, not a word."

"Is that usual?" Tink asked. "I mean, did he tell you much about his work?"

"Ed often talked about his job, especially if there was something important happening. But there was so much of his work that was just mundane and routine. He usually didn't talk about such things."

"But wouldn't he have said something about going to meet this man—the one with the information about the Alvardo brothers?"

Her mouth gave a quiver as she struggled with her emotions. "That would have been something I'd have expected him to tell me."

"Did he mention it to you, Alice?" I asked, shifting my view to her.

She shook her head. "No."

"Hmm. Who did he tell?" I asked.

"I don't know," Gladys said.

"Crumm?" Tink asked.

"Oh, I'm sure Sheriff Crumm knew about it."

"We'll talk to him later," I said. "Tell me, Mrs. Berger, did Ed seem worried about anything the day he disappeared?"

"No, not worried so much," she replied thoughtfully. "But he did seem . . . distracted. He sometimes gets that way when he's working on a problem."

"A problem?" Tink asked.

"You know, when you try to put pieces of the puzzle together. Being Rangers, I'm sure you must do the same thing."

I nodded and smiled. "Yes, ma'am. That seems to be a big part of our job."

"Did you see the letter?" Tink wondered.

"No. He never showed it to me."

I said, "Have you looked for it since Ed's disappearance?"

"No."

"Would you?"

"Yes, if you think it's important."

"It may be," I said.

Alice made us tea, and we sat in the parlor

269

while Gladys went off to search for the elusive letter.

My eyes kept going back to Alice, and I thought it was funny, but suddenly I couldn't recall Alice's face as ever being any different than the lovely face now peering wide-eyed at me over the rim of her teacup.

"I've often wondered what ever happened to you, Howie," she said. "You and Tink and Waldo, of course," she added quickly.

"Then one day Waldo shows up here in Elfrida," I said.

She smiled. "He seemed so much older. He wasn't drifting anymore, but knew exactly what he wanted." Her voice lowered, and she glanced around the room. "I never told anyone how we broke him out of jail. Remember?"

Tink and I grinned.

"Good thing. We were pretty crazy kids," Tink said.

"What have you two been doing since then?"

"It wasn't long after we dropped you off here with your aunt and uncle that we got hired on as Rangers," I said. "That sort of changed our lives for the better."

"And it came just in time," Tink added. "We were headed down the wrong road, that's for sure."

"Tink's engaged," I said, anxious to get off the subject of our past.

"Really? Who's the lucky girl?"

"Howie's sister, Anne. She's known me most of her life." Tink grinned. "And she still wants to marry me!"

Alice laughed, turning her eyes back to me. "And you, Howie?"

"I'm still single."

"No prospects?" she asked, lifting her eyebrows.

"No, no prospects. Oh, I know lots of girls, but none that I'm smitten enough to want to spend the rest of my life with."

"You're just being too picky, Howie."

"Maybe. But I'll know the right girl when I meet her." Inexplicably my eye caught hers at just that moment. A lump rose in my throat and my cheeks began to burn. I had to ask the question that had been heavy upon me ever since hearing the news from Sheriff Crumm. "Why are you marrying Waldo?" I blurted it out. Almost at once I realized how forward such a question must sound.

"Shouldn't I?" she asked.

There were a hundred reasons I could think of why she shouldn't, but none I could tell her.

"I . . . I was just wondering," I stammered suddenly, wishing I hadn't asked the question.

271

Douglas Hirt

Gladys Berger returned to rescue me from an uneasy situation. And I knew by the expression on her tired face that she had not located the damn letter.

272

Chapter Twenty-one

Sheriff Crumm and some of the men in town had gone out to look for Ed Berger right after his disappearance, but they had found no sign of him. "His horse never left the stable," Crumm told us, looking puzzled, "so wherever it was he'd gone off to, it was near enough for a man to get to afoot."

"That ought to narrow the search considerably. And you never saw the letter either?" The missing letter was beginning to gnaw at me.

"No. Ed didn't show it to me."

"Seems to me the only person who actually saw the letter was Waldo Fritz," I said. "Unless you know of someone else."

He shook his head. "I'm reckoning that Ed wanted to keep this meeting under his hat."

"Then why tell Waldo?"

"Sometimes a man's got to talk to somebody about what's on his mind. Ed just figured that Waldo would listen without trying to change his mind or insist on coming along like another lawman might—or like a wife might insist upon."

"Makes sense," Tink allowed.

I frowned and shook my head. It wasn't making sense to me. "Mind if Tink and I go through Ed's desk?"

"Sure, but you won't find anything but the usual government paperwork and some Wanted posters. I've already checked."

I wanted to get my hands on that letter. I don't know why it seemed so important. It just did.

"Where is the telegrapher's office?" I asked him.

"Up the street and around the corner to the left about four doors up. You can't miss it."

"Thanks." I said to Tink, "Start going through Ed's papers. I'm going to send off a telegram to the captain."

"Right," Tink said, taking a seat in Berger's desk chair and studying all the pigeonholes, drawers, and ledger slots.

I went up the street to the Western Union Office and sent off my inquiry to Captain Wheeler. I told the man behind the window that when he had a reply, he could find me either at the sheriff's office or at Ed Berger's house.

Outside on the boardwalk I stopped to watch a sputtering Ford chugging its way up the street, filling the air with an evil odor, its wheels wobbling around the chuckholes. The man hunched over the tiller had his teeth clenched to keep them from rattling, and his face was set in such a determined manner that I had to wonder why anyone would want to own one of those things. I doubted these newfangled horseless buggies would ever be more than just a fad for the well-to-do.

"Howie."

I wheeled about at the sound of my name. Alice had just stepped out of a grocery store a few feet away. She had a basket over her arm with bundles of fresh green vegetables peeking out of it.

"Shopping?" I asked, strolling over to her side.

"I had to pick up a few things for Gladys. She's not feeling up to shopping right now."

"I can understand that." We started to walk. I said, "It seems the Bergers took you in and treated you like their own."

"I became the daughter they never had. They couldn't have loved me any more if I'd been born to them."

275

"I worried a little about that when we were bringing you to them."

She glanced up. "You never showed it."

"I didn't want to worry you, Alice. You'd already been through so much."

"But it doesn't surprise me," she said. "You were always the one most concerned about me."

"We all cared for you, Alice."

"I knew that. But you each did so in your own way. Tink, he just tried to make a joke of everything. He made me laugh, and that helped when I was sad. Waldo, he was always in control. I sort of felt safe with him because I knew he'd be able to handle any trouble that came up."

"Yep, that was Waldo, all right." We were headed more or less in the direction of her house. "And what about me?"

Alice stopped, peering into my eyes. "You, Howie. You were the most concerned of all. Not about making me laugh or keeping me safe, although you wanted those things for me too. You were worried about me. About how I felt. You wanted to heal that hurting part inside me. When you held me in your arms I somehow knew I was going to be all right."

I felt my cheeks burn again. "You were just a little kid."

"I'm not a little kid anymore, Howie."

"You have Waldo to hold you now, Alice," I replied, trying not to sound bitter about it.

"Yes." He voice grew distant. "But he doesn't—not like he really means it. Waldo is always making plans, wanting to be successful and popular."

I nodded and had to smile. "You're right again. That's Waldo, all right."

"Why did you three split up?" she asked suddenly. "Waldo told me that it had happened, but he didn't seem to want to talk about it."

My thoughts went back to that day when we'd discovered that Waldo had been swindling us out of our share of the loot. His final words to us rang in my ears as if they had been only yesterday: *You can't walk out on me like this. You two will be sorry, I promise you!*

If Alice really loved Waldo, I didn't want to say anything to poison that. I certainly couldn't tell her about the Apache Mining Company robbery, or all the other little things that finally led up to the end.

"We just started drifting apart, Alice. Waldo wanted to do things that Tink and I didn't."

We strolled along the sidewalk. I was listening to the sound of my boots on the boards, trying to sort out my feelings, which at the moment were a confused mess. I was feeling lower than a gopher hole, yet on the other hand, just being side by side with Alice gave me a thrill like I'd never felt before.

"When is the date?" My breath caught as I waited for her reply.

"Next month. We'd just set the date when father disappeared."

My chest squeezed. "That's . . . that's great, Alice."

"Do you mean that?"

"No."

Alice stopped and looked up at me. There was a glint of light in those captivating brown eyes an instant before she turned away and started walking again. The five minutes of silence that followed as I escorted her back to her house were the hardest five minutes I'd ever endured— harder even than the time I'd told Ma and Pa I was leaving with Tink and Waldo. I wondered if I'd offended her—if I'd been too quick and forward with my reply. But it would have been impossible for me to have lied to her.

Standing there on her front porch, I fought for something to say, something to correct my mistake. I could see that like me, Alice had withdrawn into herself. "Well, I'm . . . I'm awfully glad we happened to run into each other again, Alice."

"It didn't just happen by accident, Howie."

"What do you mean?"

"I can see the sheriff's office from our kitchen window. I saw you going up the street." She made an attempt at a smile, then rushed inside.

"Any luck?" I asked.

Tink glanced up from the desk, where a half-dozen tiny drawers hung open. An instant before, his nose had been buried in the pile of papers that spilled over the green, leather desk pad, half burying an inkwell and the base of a green-shaded electric lamp.

"And we thought the Rangers had a lot of useless paperwork to push around!" he snorted as he riffled the pile in front of him.

I was still unsettled by my "chance" encounter with Alice, but I forced a smile anyway and pulled around a chair to lend a hand.

"You can tackle that drawer." He toed one of the larger ones that hung open.

I made room on the desk and hauled out a folder filled with what looked like letters and dispatches from the government.

"What do you expect to learn by finding that letter?" Sheriff Crumm asked at one point, craning his neck over the top of the desk and peering down on our mess.

"I don't know," I said. "It just would be nice to actually see the thing and read for ourselves what it said."

"Mr. Fritz already told you what it said." Crumm scratched absentmindedly at his neck.

"Yeah, I know." I wasn't about to let on to Crumm the low level of regard I had for Waldo's integrity. That could open the door to more questions than I'd care to answer.

Crumm wandered back to his desk, and a moment later a long yawn punctuated the sound of Tink and me rattling the papers. We went through every scrap in and on the desk, and after working at it an hour or so, we put it all away as we had found it and sat there looking at each other.

"Nothing." I sucked in a bit of my cheek and chewed at it, wondering what our next move would be.

"He must've had it on him after all." Tink seemed to have resigned himself to the obvious.

"I reckon it's back to Waldo. He's the only lead we have."

"Yeah. Maybe he'll remember something else."

I gave a short laugh. "Waldo will remember only as much as Waldo wants to remember."

Tink rolled his eyes. "I'll bet he's just waiting for someone to offer a reward."

"I wouldn't put it past him." I put my chair back behind the other desk and snatched up my hat. Tink turned to leave, and I was about to follow on his heels when something caught my eye.

I looked back and considered Marshal Berger's desktop. Everything was as it had been when we first arrived, except . . . I had missed it before, but that green desk pad was resting kind of crooked, as if there was something beneath it. I lifted a corner of it and removed a large piece of paper folded into quarters.

It was an old Wanted poster by its size and feel. Tink had come back, and he gave me a questioning look. I unfolded the paper and pressed it flat upon the desktop. It must have been hanging somewhere near a window for a long time, for most of it was sun-faded. It was the old poster of Waldo from the time we'd held up the Apache Mining Company payroll—the one with half his face covered by a bandana.

Marshal Berger had taken a pencil to the poster and had sketched out the missing portion of it—right down to the thin mustache Waldo was wearing these days!

"He knew," Tink whispered. "Berger knew."

I nodded and cast a cautious glance at Crumm, but the sheriff was busy sawing logs and hadn't heard. I refolded the poster, slipped it under my vest, and left.

We walked up the street, around the corner, and down an alley where we could talk without unwanted ears turning our way. I unfolded that poster again for a better look.

"What do you make of it, Howie?"

"It looks like Berger had a spark of inspiration and played a hunch."

"He must've had that thing hanging around for years. Probably looked at it every day, trying to figure out who it was behind that mask. Wonder how long he knew. What tipped him off?"

I shrugged. "Waldo comes back to town. Waldo starts courting his stepdaughter. Maybe Waldo flashed around some cash—he bought that saloon, after all. Berger, being the dutiful father he is, begins to check up on his future son-in-law—just to be on the safe side."

"Sure, that's got to be it." Tink grimaced. "Big problem for Waldo until Alvardo comes looking for the marshal. I wonder if Waldo knew the marshal was on to him. I wonder if he had a hand in helping Alvardo set the marshal up."

Alvardo? I'd almost worked him out of the picture. I frowned. "I think the time has come to pay Waldo another visit."

"What do you have in mind?"

"He's the only one around who seems to have seen that letter, and he knew where Berger was planning to meet this elusive stranger who wanted fifty dollars to squeal on Alvardo."

I carefully tucked the poster back inside my

shirt. We emerged into the sunlight again and crossed the street to the Crystal Slipper Saloon.

"Hey! Mr. Fritz says he's not to be disturbed," the thick, ruddy-faced bartender barked at Tink and me as we marched around the tables and to the door. I tried the handle. It was locked.

"What do you want?" Waldo demanded from the other side.

"It's us, Waldo. Open this door."

There were some hurried footsteps. I nodded, and Tink turned into a hallway and disappeared.

There was some scuffling beyond the door a moment later, then a key turned and Waldo's dark eyes flashed in the opening. They flicked away from me and scowled viciously at Tink, who had come through the back door and was gripping the arm of a woman in a beaded dress.

"You better have a good reason," Waldo growled, stepping aside to let me in.

I closed the door behind me, and Tink let go of the woman. She glowered at him, rubbing her arm. "What the hell is this all about, Waldie?"

Waldo's scowl deepened. "Get out of here."

Pouting, the woman snatched a smoldering cigarette from the ashtray on his desk, tossed her head, and marched out the back door.

Waldo was shaking with rage. He managed to

draw in a long breath and forcibly calmed himself. "What is it now, Blake?"

"Bad form, isn't it . . . *Waldie?*"

His eyes narrowed dangerously.

"A man engaged to be married, entertaining a whore in his private quarters?"

"You didn't come here because of her."

"The letter. Where is it?"

"How should I know?"

"It seems you are the only one in town who had a chance to see it."

"Is that a crime? I'm just lucky, I guess." Waldo strode to his desk and fumbled a cigarette from its silver case. He thrust it between his thin lips and put a match to it. Blowing out a cloud of smoke, he speared me with another narrow look. "I already told you all I know. Now it's up to you Rangers to find Berger. I'm out of it."

"Not quite, bucko." Tink gave me a nod.

I tossed Waldo the poster, and it fell at his feet.

"What's this?"

"Open it up," Tink said.

Waldo glanced at him, then me, and bent for it, unfolding the poster as he straightened. His face tightened and his eyes shot up.

"Where did you get this?"

"If I recollect right, you always did want your picture on a Wanted poster, Waldo. Well, there you have it. Pretty true likeness, especially after the marshal finished in the lower half."

"I don't know anything about this."

"Don't you?" Tink pushed away from the doorjamb where he'd been leaning and came across to my side of the room. "Makes me have to wonder if Alvardo didn't have a helping hand in the marshal's disappearance."

"That's stupid. You're stupid, Tink."

Tink clucked disapprovingly and shook his head. "You can do better than that, *Waldie*."

"Let's assume you didn't know," I said. "It's a safe bet Berger already had his eye on you. Maybe you started getting suspicious by the way he was acting."

"No."

"All right. Tell me where he went."

Waldo was shaken. I'd never seen him that way before.

"It's no secret. He was supposed to meet him at the old Maria Valdez mining camp. About ten miles south east of here."

"Ten miles?"

Tink gave a low whistle. "That's a heck of a walk."

"What do you mean?" Waldo demanded.

Douglas Hirt

I took the poster from him and tucked it into my shirt. "We'll be seeing you, Waldo."

We left him standing there confused, worried—and, perhaps for the first time in his life, not knowing what to do next.

Chapter Twenty-two

It was too late in the day to head out to the mining camp, so we swung by the Western Union office. There was still no reply to my telegram to Captain Wheeler. Sheriff Crumm was outside the jailhouse, locking the door, when Tink and I strolled up.

"Oh, you've come back."

"Closing up shop?" Tink grinned.

"Yep. Say, you boys got a place to sleep tonight?"

"We haven't thought that far ahead," I said.

He nodded at the door he'd just locked. "We have no customers inside, so if you'd like to bunk in on the cots, you're welcome."

"Thanks. That'll be fine," I said.

Crumm unlocked the door, and we went inside. The late-afternoon light slanted through one of the windows, landing brightly on the desk that Tink and I had searched a little earlier.

"I'm going to be out of the office tomorrow," Crumm said, pulling open a drawer in his desk and feeling around inside it. "But you boys are welcome to use it if you need to." He found an extra key and handed it to Tink. "Just make sure you lock the place up if you intend to be away for a long time."

"We will. Thanks." Tink shoved the key into his vest pocket.

"Well, you boys have a good night." Crumm started for the door. "Oh, almost forgot. Miss Haynes was by a little while ago looking for you two. She's invited you two to dinner tonight." An inquiring look crossed his face. "You know her from somewhere, don't you—and you know Mr. Fritz too, right?"

I nodded. "We know them both from way back." Crumm was anxious for more details, but I only smiled. "Thanks for the use of your jail tonight. We'll take good care of it."

"Yeah, sure. Well, good night." He hid his disappointment and left.

"Dinner!" Tink beamed. "Elfrida is looking more and more like a good town."

I laughed. "You always did do more thinking with your belly than your head, Tink."

"A man's got to keep his priorities in order."

We showed up on Alice's doorstep around seven o'clock and were promptly ushered into the small, tidy house. Gladys did her best to be hospitable, with Alice there to help her over the rough places. It was plain that both these women were under a lot of stress. Ed Berger had been missing almost two weeks, and that didn't bode well—and they knew it. Gladys was setting out the plates when she suddenly stopped and glanced up, counting heads.

"Where's Waldo, dear?" she asked distractedly. Her thoughts had been somewhere else.

"He said he had something important to do tonight. Business. He won't be able to make dinner."

Business? I had detected a note of bitterness in her voice. Then I caught Tink's smirk.

Waldo's important business, I reckoned, was keeping out of Tink's and my way.

Over dinner, I told Alice and Gladys about our plans to ride out to the old Maria Valdez mines in the morning to look for clues.

"I pray you'll find Ed, and that he's all right," Gladys said, her eyes filling.

Alice gently patted her hand.

"Tink and me, we're going to do all we can, Mrs. Berger," I promised, putting a positive spin on it even though I didn't hold out much hope of finding anything. Crumm and his deputies had already checked out that abandoned mining camp and come up empty-handed.

Afterward, with the table cleared, we went out front on the porch, where a pleasant night breeze was stirring the leaves of the old cottonwood tree. Gladys spoke of Elfrida, and how it had grown so since they had first moved in, but when she mentioned something about Ed, it became too painful to continue and she excused herself and went back inside the house.

Alice tried not to let it show, but her concerns over Ed were pressing hard against her, too heavy to fully hide. She spoke of her life after we'd left her, of how Gladys and Ed had taken her into their hearts. I could have listened to Alice all night. I was intrigued by the way the lamplight through the window sculpted the side of her face and glinted in those quick, wide eyes.

Tink told her all about Anne, and afterward I think he was lonesome for her, because he grew mighty quiet, his thoughts straying from the thread of the conversation. Finally he yawned and announced that he was heading back to the sheriff's office for some shut-eye. He poked his head inside the house to give his regards to Gladys, then, tipping his hat at Alice, he strolled off into the night, calling, "I'll leave the door unlocked for you, Howie."

Alice and I talked for another hour or two, of nothing in particular, our words glancing off a wagonload of unrelated topics, but each somehow bringing us closer. We took a stroll around the block before I left, enjoying the quiet and coolness of the night—and just being together.

I'd once told Tink that when I found the right girl I'd somehow know it. When Alice and I parted later, something had changed inside both of us.

Tink and I stopped by the Western Union office the next morning before heading out of town. The telegrapher shook his head upon seeing us enter, and I said I'd swing by later.

The road south hadn't changed any since the last time Tink, Waldo, and I had ridden it. Once Elfrida was behind us, an empty land stretched out in all directions, with a haze of mountains looming far to our left.

Tink said, "Know what day today is?"

I shrugged. "Wednesday?"

"Your birthday."

I pulled to a stop and stared at him, amazed. "You're right. I completely forgot about that."

Tink grinned. "You just have too much on your mind right now."

"Boy, ain't that the truth." We started riding again.

"I didn't get you a present yet," Tink went on.

"Don't need to, Tink."

"But I want to. When we get back to town I'll go shopping."

I let it drop, but I couldn't help but remember that the first time I'd set eyes on Waldo Fritz, it had been on my birthday. I'd done a lot of growing up since then, and so had Tink.

About five miles along the road we came upon the turnoff we'd been looking for. I dismounted, kicked around among the sagebrush, and turned over an ancient wooden sign that had once pointed the way to the Maria Valdez Mining Company. The cracked and weathered boards, half buried by blowing dirt, now pointed to nowhere.

"This is the turnoff, all right," I said, swinging back onto my saddle. "Just where the stableman said it would be."

We followed the little-used rutted road back into some low hills. It had been a dry season, and what prints had been left behind remained in the ground for a long time. Mixed in among the occasional hoofprints were the distinct tire marks of an automobile. I'd never trailed an automobile before, and I discovered it was a lot easier than tracking a man on horse.

Soon a cluster of dilapidated buildings appeared out of a hillside ahead. We rode in amongst them where the ground was pocked with a dozen scattered mounds of rock, stained yellow and rusted from the occasional rains. There were maybe the same number of deep pit mines, like the one that Alice nearly fell into years ago. The wooden buildings were the color of the land around them, while the curling tin roofs were rusty red. Where the winds had folded back a corner, old timber skeletons showed beneath. There was a hoist shack with all its machinery still in place, and a head frame over one particularly large hole. The other buildings had been the mine offices, toolsheds and storage, and living quarters for the men who were long gone from this place.

"What are we looking for?" Tink asked as we led our horses into the shade of one of the buildings.

"I'm not sure." I briefly scanned the ghost camp. "But if Ed met someone here, maybe he left something behind. Something that can tell us where he went."

"You're playing a long shot, Howie."

"You take them as they come. So far a long shot is the only shot we have."

We went off in different directions, first checking out the old living quarters, then searching the work shacks. There had been a lot of garbage left behind when the company pulled out, and maybe that would work to our advantage. Anything dropped more recently would stand out against the faded clutter . . . or maybe it would just be lost among it. As Tink had said, it was a long shot.

We spent the morning kicking around the place, and other than a few hoofprints and the automobile tracks, we didn't find anything. Frustrated, Tink and I regrouped near the old hoist shack and put our heads together.

"Wonder which one of those machine we saw back in town made these tracks," I said, toeing a tire print at my feet.

"We can ask around," Tink suggested.

"Whoever it was, he probably came with Crumm when the sheriff checked out this place."

"I'll wager it was Waldo's machine what made them." Tink hunkered down and traced the tread mark with his finger. "You think there is enough difference in tire tracks to tell one machine from another?"

"Maybe. To someone who knew what they were looking for."

"Hmm. I wonder . . ." Tink stood and followed the tire tracks down past the old head frame to a place where they suddenly stopped. Here the tracks reversed themselves in a way that looked as if the machine had been turned around by backing it up and then coming forward again. From this point the machine took a slightly different path back to the road.

"What do you make of it, Tink?"

"I don't know." His brow wrinkled as he grabbed the rusty hoist cable and leaned out over the gaping pit beneath the head frame. I waited against the creosoted timbers, wondering what he had in mind. Tink started around the wide hole and then stopped to sniff the air two or three times. Then he walked to the far side. Going to his knees, he grabbed the shoring timbers and stared long and hard into the blackness below.

"What is it?"

He looked up at me, but his view seemed to be elsewhere. His eyes compressed as he stood and came back around.

"What did Waldo say back then?"

"Back when?"

"That night when we almost lost Alice. Afterward, when we were sitting around the campfire talking."

I shrugged. "Heck, Tink. I don't know. That was a long time ago."

"Yeah, but when he said it, I remember how you and I looked at each other. He'd said something like how that mine shaft would have been a convenient place to lose a body. Remember?"

I frowned, searching my memory. And then there it was, vaguely coming back to me now that Tink had mentioned it. "I recall now," I narrowed my eyes at Tink, "but you don't think . . ."

Tink's face went stone sober. "Take a whiff."

I moved carefully down to the edge and inhaled the draft of air rising from the pit mine. Mixed in it was the faint odor of decay.

"One of us has to go down there," I said, scrambling back from the precipice.

Tink tossed a rock, and we listened to the distant clatter. "It's not that deep. A hundred feet or so."

Between the two of us we carried about a hundred and fifty feet of rope on our saddles. Tying them together, Tink made one end fast to the head frame and tossed the other over the edge.

"I'll go," I said, slipping on a pair of leather gloves.

"You sure, Howie? You don't like heights."

I didn't, and I shuddered remembering how I'd rescued Alice and nearly plunged over the edge of that mine shaft while attempting it. But this was something I felt I just had to do.

"Got any matches?"

Tink hurried back to his horse and returned with a handful of stick matches. Wrapping the rope once around my waist and twice about my gloved hand, I lowered myself over the edge, feeling for a toehold in the shoring timbers below. Working my way down into the cool mine shaft, I could feel the square of daylight shrink above me as the inky gloom closed in from below. The stench of death grew heavier as I descended. Taking my time and feeling for niches with my toes, I lowered myself deeper and deeper. I was beginning to worry that I'd run out of rope before hitting bottom when suddenly my feet came down on a sloping, rocky surface.

The foul smell was nearly overpowering. I tried to breathe shallowly, but as winded as I was from the climb, that was impossible. Far above, Tink's face was a speck in a tiny patch of blue. Not daring to let go of the rope, I fished a match from my pocket and struck it against the rocky wall. The light flared, showing me that I'd indeed reached bottom. Some twisted metal and a broken shovel lay at my feet. Over in one corner was a small dog-size skeleton. I held the match high and turned. Just before it guttered, I spied a dark shape in the other corner.

My chest squeezed in that instant before the match went out. I'd seen another body. Untangling myself from the rope, I struck another light and made my way across the uneven ground. It was a man, twisted as if his neck and back had been broken. The stench nearly overpowered me. I couldn't see a face, only the dark, bloated form. A vest was stretched taut over the corpse. I didn't want to touch it, but I had to do it. I had to know for certain. Grabbing hold, I gave a tug.

The body rolled, and Marshal Ed Berger's ghastly face looked up at me. Instinctively I took a step backward. There were no eyes, only the sunken lids. Something was moving. I looked closer. Maggots writhed in the empty sockets. His skin had begun to slough off in powder-white flakes. Insects had gotten to him bad.

The sight turned my stomach. Then the match kissed my fingertips. I dropped it and struck another. It was impossible to determine the cause of death. Whether it was by the fall, or whether Ed Berger been dead before, only a coroner might be able to tell now, and even that was doubtful. I caught a glimpse of his badge still pinned to the vest. Removing it, I slipped it into my pocket, then backed away, reaching for the rope. But then I remembered the letter. I had to find it. Kneeling at his side, I searched through his pockets, lighting a third and then a fourth match.

"What didya find, Howie?" Tink shouted down.

I couldn't tell him, not yet, not from down here in the stench. A deep ache filled my heart. I regretted Berger's death, but more than that, I was grieving for Alice and Gladys. I dropped the match, took a hold on the rope, and started that long, slow climb back to daylight.

Chapter Twenty-three

"Alvardo lured the marshal out to those shacks, murdered him, then dumped his body down that mine shaft," Tink surmised as we rode back to Elfrida. "Somehow he must have got the drop on the marshal. Maybe he bushwhacked him from one of those buildings. It would have been easy."

"How do you explain the wheel tracks?" I was piecing it together in another way, and I didn't like the way the picture was beginning to shape up. But there was still absolutely no proof. If Alvardo did it, he was long gone, and although Waldo was unscrupulous, I couldn't see him murdering the marshal.

"Maybe Alvardo bought himself a machine," Tink suggested. "Or maybe, like we already talked about, it was Waldo's, or someone else's who came up looking for the marshal."

"A man who just busted out of prison? Where would he get the money for one of them machines?"

Tink's eyes compressed thoughtfully. "But it would explain why those tracks led straight to *that* particular mine shaft. There were at least a dozen others around. If the machine had belonged to someone in the search party, it's doubtful he would have stopped right there. You can push coincidence only so far, Howie."

I had to laugh. "That coming from a man who managed to stumble into two robberies-in-progress while planning to commit one himself!"

Tink's mouth slanted in a halfhearted grin. "Yeah, that was sorta a coincidence, wasn't it?"

"I'd call it so."

He shook his head. "We may never know what happened. Alvardo's probably clear down to South America by now."

"That's where I'd be," I said as we came into town.

"And what do you make of the letter still missing?" he asked.

"Ranger Blake."

We had been passing by the Western Union office. The telegrapher came out onto the boardwalk, holding an envelope in his hand. "Got that reply you've been waiting for."

Tink and I turned into the hitching rail, and he handed it up to me. "Hope it's the answer you're looking for," he said, standing there.

"Me too." I ripped the flap and extracted the telegram. A scowl cut into my forehead.

"What's wrong?" Tink asked worriedly.

"I reckon this does answer our question." I handed the paper across to Tink.

Tink's lips moved silently with the words. Stunned as I had been, his eyes leaped up. "A farmer shot him trying to steal a horse? Three weeks ago? In South Dakota!"

"That would make it about a week before Marshal Berger was murdered. How does a dead man lure Marshal Berger out of town, then bushwhack him?"

"Berger? The marshal is dead?" the telegrapher asked, a look of astonishment in his suddenly wide eyes.

I nodded, then reined my horse around and rode away. We let ourselves inside the sheriff's office with the key and I flung the telegram onto Berger's desk.

"Where does this leave us now, Howie?"

"With a dead marshal and only one man with reason enough to kill him."

"We can't prove Waldo did it. Maybe it was

someone else. Maybe the man who wrote that letter did it after all."

"There is no letter. Never was." I drew my revolver and thumbed open the loading gate, slipping a sixth bullet into the hole that I usually left open for safety.

"What are you going to do?"

I was staring at the gun, recalling the afternoon that I'd taken it from Waldo. If I had arrested him then and there, Ed Berger would still be alive. My life would have changed. I'd have been kicked out of the Rangers and maybe sent to jail, but at least Berger would be alive!

"I'm bringing him in, Tink."

"Wait a minute. Let's think this through. We still have no proof, Howie. And anyway, you going busting in there with that thing is just asking for a fight."

"He murdered Ed! The father of the woman he intends to marry. How can a man do that? I let Waldo go once when I could have put him behind bars. It's my fault Berger is dead. This is something I have to do!"

Tink's face cast itself in stone for a moment, then his eyes widened slowly. "This isn't so much about Ed as it is about Alice, isn't it?"

"You saw them, the way they're being all twisted up inside not knowing if Ed is alive or dead. Now we've got to tell them. It's going to tear them up. And the man responsible is someone they trust. He's betrayed them both. Waldo is probably betraying Alice again right now with that painted floozy he entertains in his quarters!"

"Howie, just hold up a minute. You're thinking with your heart, not your head. Maybe what you say is all true, but if you go against Waldo, he'll kill you! You know how he is with a gun. You're no match for him. Shoot, Howie, even I'm better with a gun than you are. This is suicide!"

"I've got to go after him, Tink."

"I can't let you! You're not thinking straight, Howie. Let's you and me go talk to him."

"I'm done talking." I started for the door.

Tink grabbed me by the shirtsleeve.

Maybe Tink was right. Maybe I was thinking with my heart instead of my head. All I knew was, I was furious at the thought of what Waldo had done to Alice. I was furious at myself. And I was furious at Tink for trying to stop me. Sudden anger blinded me, and I rounded on him.

Tink saw it coming. He ducked under my bunched knuckles and danced to one side. I stabbed out with another jab, missing him again.

In my fury I didn't see his fist. It seemed to come out of nowhere, and my teeth crashed together as my head snapped around. I staggered back against Berger's desk. The room swirled and went out of focus as I slumped toward the floor. Tink caught me before I hit. Only half aware of what was happening, I felt my heels dragging along the floor. Then I was lying flat on something soft. Distantly came the squeal of iron against iron, then a solid clank.

I lay there stunned for a few seconds while the room slowly stopped spinning and finally steadied. My eyes cleared, and I found myself staring out at the sheriff's office through a grid of flat, iron bars. Shaking the last of the fog from my brain, I leaped off the cot and rattled the jail cell's door. It was locked, and Tink was gone. The ring of keys sat on Sheriff Crumm's desk, well beyond my reach.

"Tink!" I yelled. "Tink!"

I wheeled around and grabbed for the window bars, pressing my cheek hard against them so I could see up the street. Tink was just turning the corner onto the main street.

"Tink! Come back here!"

With sudden rage I jerked at the bars, but Samson wasn't my name, and unlike the pillars of the temple of Dagon, they remained firmly rooted in the solid brick wall. I turned back to the locked door, becoming aware of the pain spreading through my jaw. Cocking my jaw side to side, I determined that it wasn't broken.

"Damn!" I slammed my hand flat against the iron lock plate, sending a wave of pain up my arm. "Dammit, Tink, what do you think you are doing?"

For a long moment I stood clinging to the bars. Then the distant sounds of voices drew me back to the window. From my vantage point, I had only a narrow view of Elfrida's main street, but I could tell the sounds were coming from that direction. People were moving up the street as if being drawn to something happening beyond my angle of view, pointing as they went.

Then suddenly the office door flew open and Alice rushed in. She stopped, glanced around the vacant room, and seeing that no one was there, started back outside.

"Alice!"

Her head snapped around. "Howie?"

I saw the tears streaming down her cheeks as she rushed across the floor to me. "What—" she started, then stopped suddenly.

"The keys. On Crumm's desk. Get them!"

She searched a moment, then grabbed up the big ring. "Is it true? Did you find . . . Father? Is he . . ." She couldn't bring herself to say the word.

I frowned and nodded.

Her tears came in a flood. I reached through

the bars and pulled her tight to me. "I'm sorry, Alice. I was going to tell you, but . . ." A thought occurred to me then. "How did you find out so soon? We just got back into town."

"Bill Denton, the telegrapher, told someone and the word spread."

A sudden fear gripped me. "If you've heard already, then surely Waldo—" I rushed back to the window and saw more men hurrying up the street.

"Tink!"

Waldo knew, and he'd be waiting for Tink! I reached through the bars and grabbed the key from her hand. In a heartbeat I had the cell door open.

"What?" Alice asked, following on my heels.

"Tink's gone after Waldo!"

"Waldo? But why?"

I didn't have time to tell her what I'd discovered, but in that instant she must have read the truth in my face.

"No. He didn't!"

I nodded, then turned out the front door, putting on a burst of speed. I flew up the side street, praying I wasn't too late. Alice was somewhere behind me, encumbered by her long skirts and unable to keep up. I skidded around the corner and drew up all at once, my heart pounding. Two blocks up, Tink and Waldo were standing in the street with a crowd of people lining either side of the dusty track. They seemed to be talking, but I couldn't hear their words. I was about to call out, when suddenly Waldo's hand shot for the gun in his holster. He snapped it out like lightning, and the boom reverberated in the air. Tink spun away and fell facefirst into the street. His hand had never even gotten close to his gun.

"Tink!" I cried. Catching my breath, I leaped off the boardwalk and raced up the street, slumping to my knees at his side. I blinked back sudden moisture and right then hardly noticed the desert wind, or the dust that stung my eyes.

"Tink!" I put an arm under him and pulled his head up onto my legs. My hand was suddenly warm, and when I looked, blood dripped through my fingers. Out the corner of my eye I saw Alice running up the boardwalk. She stopped abruptly and clutched at the porch upright as if her knees had gone weak. The hot wind had pulled her hair loose and whipped it across her wide, staring eyes. There was horror in her face, and she must have seen the same in mine as I looked back at the man in my arms.

"Tink," I tried again. There was no response at first, then his eyes fluttered and came open. They seemed not to see me.

"Tink, I'm here."

"I . . . I know," he managed. "Did . . . did I get him?"

My glance went down the street. Waldo Fritz hadn't moved. Tall and still slender after all these years, Waldo's gaunt face grinned at me as he slowly slipped his revolver back into its holster. He took an unlit cigar from an inside pocket of his frock coat and turned it between his lips. He seemed to be waiting.

I looked back at my friend and shook my head.

Tink coughed, and his eyes rolled up some. "Not surprised . . . Waldo always faster than me . . . than you . . ."

"Why did you do it?"

He half grinned. "You know why, Howie. It's . . . it's always been my job, watching after you," he wheezed.

"Don't talk." I glared into the crowd beginning to gather around. "Someone get a doctor!"

Tink clutched my arm with a sudden urgency. "Too late for that." His eyes shifted toward Alice. "She's a good woman, Howie. Don't . . . don't let Waldo ruin her with his . . ." A ragged cough carried off the rest of what he wanted to say. When it passed, a smile moved across Tink's blanched lips. "I'm gonna be all right— soon. You . . . you take care, old friend. . . . Lousy birthday present . . . sorry. This definitely is not a good town," he rasped as his eyes closed.

I gently laid Tink's head on the ground and turned toward Waldo.

"Your move, Howie," he said evenly, grinning around that cigar in his mouth.

"This is what you had in mind all along, isn't it?" I stepped away from Tink, facing Waldo in the middle of the road. "You promised you'd get even with us all those years ago. And this is how you planned to do it. Killing Ed Berger was only the bait to get us here."

His voice turned suddenly low and hard. "For some men, revenge is everything." Waldo's dark eyes narrowed ever so slightly as the grin faded from his gaunt face. "I didn't want it to happen that way, but Berger figured out it was me who held up that payroll. He must have known you and Tink were partners in it too. I couldn't let him ruin everything I've built here." Waldo seemed unconcerned now that his own words were condemning him here in front of all these people.

The crowds had thickened along both sides of the road. Out the corner of my eye, I saw that Alice had gone to Tink and was bending over him.

Waldo's grin returned, and casually his hand

dipped inside his jacket for a match. "I need a smoke."

I inclined my head toward Alice. "If your bullet goes wide, you'll hit her."

"My shots never go wide, Howie. You know that."

I was sweating. I took a handkerchief from my pocket and mopped my head. "Just the same, I'd appreciate it if you let me move a few steps off to the side."

He held up the match with his thumb poised on the head and bowed graciously toward me. "Move if you wish, Howie."

I shifted two or three steps to my right. Some of the people down the street scrambled aside now that my back was toward them. I mopped my head again and pushed the handkerchief deep into my pocket.

Waldo's thumb flicked fire to the match.

At that instant I dropped to the ground and pulled out the derringer as I hit. I'd already cocked it in my pocket. As I knew he would, as soon as that match flared, Waldo's hand stabbed for his revolver.

But I was a split second ahead of him. I aimed the little pistol and fired.

Waldo spun to the left. His gun snapped out of the holster and fired, cutting a furrow in the dirt alongside my arm. I fired again. Waldo lurched backward, stumbled, and collapsed.

Leaping to my feet, I drew my revolver and covered him. But Waldo wasn't moving. Cautiously, I stepped near and kicked the revolver away from his open fingers. A spot of red had begun to spread across the middle of his white shirt. I lowered myself cautiously alongside him.

"Waldo?"

The crowd rushed off the sidewalk and gathered around. Waldo's breathing was shallow, but then his eyes opened and found me.

"How—how did you . . ."

"How did I beat your hand?"

He blinked and nodded.

"You're the one who taught me how to do it, Waldo. Remember? Distraction can be your best ally? Your very words. You used to preach it to us all the time. That's why I knew what you were doing when you went for that match. That's what I was doing when I used that handkerchief to mop my head. Distraction."

A faint smile touched his lips. "So you were listening, after all."

"Sure I was."

Waldo must have found something humorous in that. He laughed silently, then coughed and went still, his shining eyes, staring up at the cloudless sky, turning dull and empty.

A Good Town

"I listened," I said softly as I stood, a sudden sadness filling my heart. "I listened more than you knew, Waldo."

I loaded Alice's bags into the back of Ed Berger's buckboard some weeks later, and helped her up onto the front seat.

"Are you all ready to leave, Mrs. Blake?" I asked Alice with a grin that might have reached from Elfrida to Bisbee all by itself. *Mrs. Blake.* I sure did like the sound of that!

"I'm ready," she said, adjusting the bonnet to keep the harsh Arizona sun off her face.

Gladys reached up, and the two women had themselves a final hug. "Have a safe trip, Alice. I'll be down to visit soon as you two find a place of your own," Gladys promised.

I went around to the other side of the buckboard and climbed aboard, taking up the reins and poising my foot above the brake release. "We'll wire you soon as we get to Bisbee."

Gladys shaded her eyes with a hand. "Please do, Howie."

"I hear there are plans to run telephone wires to Bisbee," Alice said, excitement in her voice.

"That would be wonderful." Gladys glanced up at me. "You take care of my girl."

"I will." Alice smiled and squeezed my hand. "I'll take good care of her, Mrs. Berger."

313

I snapped the reins, and we started away as Gladys Berger waved good-bye from the front porch of her pink adobe house. Then we turned a corner and she was out of sight. Alice straightened around and peered ahead as we headed for the edge of town.

"Elfrida is a good town . . . to be leaving."

Alice and I both turned and glanced over our shoulders at Tink, who was grinning at us from the pallet of blankets and the pillows he was leaning against. His shirt was bulkier than usual, but that was from all the bandages wrapped about his chest.

"Oh, you think so?" Alice asked.

"Considering that I came within a cat's whisker of spending eternity here, I'm thinking it's a great place to be leaving."

I said, "You didn't like the idea of spending eternity up on boot hill next to Waldo?"

"Pl-eease." He made a sour face. "Don't remind me."

Sadness momentarily shadowed Alice's face, and I knew she was thinking of Ed . . . and Waldo. She'd had a hard time coming to grips with Ed's death and Waldo's deception.

"Yep, a good town to be leaving," Tink reiterated, making himself comfortable.

"I think Anne would agree with you on that."

"Anne." He sighed, a dreamy look and a smile

on his face as he shut his eyes. "I sure am missing her. Yep, I surely am."

I caught Alice's eye and was rewarded with one of her smiles. "Bisbee is a good town," I assured her.

"I think I am going to like it there."

"I'll make you happy."

When she gave my arm a squeeze I felt that old wanderlust leave my body. It was a worn-out ghost that would haunt me no more. I was content. Tink was alive, Alice was at my side, and a good town waited just down the road.

BRANDISH

DOUGLAS HIRT

FIRST TIME IN PAPERBACK!

Captain Ethan Brandish has finally given up his command of Fort Lowell, deep in Apache territory. But the vicious Apache leader, Yellow Shirt, has another fate in store for him. He and a group of renegade warriors attack a stage station and ride off just before Brandish arrives. But the Apaches are still out there—watching and waiting—and Brandish must risk his own life to save the few wounded survivors.

___4323-8 $4.50 US/$5.50 CAN

Dorchester Publishing Co., Inc.
P.O. Box 6640
Wayne, PA 19087-8640

Lockwood
LAURAN PAINE

In the Wyoming town of Derby, Cuff Lockwood is wounded in a gunfight and has to stay long enough to recuperate . . . and meet the pretty widow Lady Barlow, owner of the Barlow ranch. The ranch is in need of a ramrod, but Lockwood refuses the job. After all, Wyoming isn't what he had in mind. But it looks like Fate—or someone else—doesn't want Lockwood to leave town. When he tries he's ambushed and forced to stay again. It seems to Lockwood like his journey's ending, but sometimes life leads you down trails you never expected. Some mighty dangerous trails.

___4906-6 $4.50 US/$5.50 CAN